Colby Young and Diego Champagne continue to steal moments together when passion becomes so intense it cannot be denied.

Danger is ever-present as an old enemy of Diego's resurfaces and is out for vengeance. And in an attempt to convince everyone around him of his heterosexuality, Diego sleeps with Tammy, who longs to become his "old lady." His heart, however, belongs to Colby, who must swallow his own pain at the necessary deception.

Meanwhile, Diego's mother falls ill, which draws her and Colby closer as they both fret for Diego's life. And when it comes to his own family issues, Colby finally learns what happened to his little sister, which completely shatters his world.

Now, Diego walks a fine line, maintaining his leadership role and dealing with his emotions, which he sometimes finds difficult to hold in check. And when a sudden change in Colby's life threatens to pull him away from Diego forever, will the secret lovers find even a moment of true happiness?

CONTENT ADVISORY: This is a re-edited re-release title.

Transparent Moonlight
Copyright © 2019 A. J. Llewellyn and D. J. Manly
ISBN: 978-1-4874-2512-8
Cover art by Martine Jardin

Published by eXtasy Books Inc or
Devine Destinies, an imprint of eXtasy Books Inc

Look for us online at:
www.eXtasybooks.com or www.devinedestinies.com

Transparent Moonlight
Rough Riders Book 3

By

A. J. Llewellyn and D. J. Manly

DEDICATION

Four wheels move the body. Two wheels move the soul. A good rider has balance, judgment, and good timing. So does a good lover.
– Anonymous

TRADEMARKS ACKNOWLEDGEMENT

The author acknowledges the trademarked status and trademark owners of the following wordmarks mentioned in this work of fiction:

Another Broken Egg: Another Broken Egg Café

Autumn Leaves: music by Joseph Kosma; lyrics by Jacques Prevért (French) & Johnny Mercer (English)

Bates Motel: Universal City Studios LLC

Beatles: Apple Corps Limited

Best Western Plus Richmond Inn & Suites: Best Western International, Inc.

Best Western: Best Western International, Inc.

Birmingham-Shuttlesworth Airport: Birmingham Airport Authority

BMW: Bayerische Motoren Werke Aktiengesellschaft

Buick: General Motors LLC

CNN: Cable News Network, Inc.

Coca-Cola / Coke: The Coca-Cola Company

Coors Light: MillerCoors LLC

Delta: Delta Air Lines, Inc.

Disney: Disney Enterprises, Inc.

Dog the Bounty Hunter: A&E Television Networks, LLC

Dr. Oz: Oz Property Holdings, LLC

Ford: Ford Motor Company

Google: Google Inc.

iPad: Apple Inc.

Justin Timberlake: Tennman Brands, LLC

NFL: National Football League Association
Prince: Paisley Park Enterprises, Inc.
Posturepedic: Sealy Technology LLC
Red Man: Pinkerton Tobacco Co. LP
Ritz-Carlton: Ritz-Carlton Hotel Company LLC
She's So High: written by Tal Bachman
Smithsonian Institute: Smithsonian Institution Trust Instrumentality
Southern Comfort: Sazerac Brands, LLC
Trans Am: Sports Car Club of America, Incorporated
The Crying Game: Miramax Films
U.S. Marshals: Transportation Security Administration (TSA)
When Doves Cry: written by Prince

CHAPTER ONE

Diego

The day of the funeral for Dave, Jackson, and Giles was a long day. And of course, the guys wanted to party in their names back at the club later. I just wanted to crawl into a hole somewhere and sleep. It wasn't so much the funeral that had been exhausting, it was everything around it. I'd talked at length to Badger, leader of the Texas Crushers, and I was now convinced they'd had nothing to do with the attack on the clubhouse.

Since Badger had made an overture to me before I'd taken Chase's place as leader, it would have been counterproductive to attack us now.

Cledus, Colby's father, despised the Texas Crushers. He just kept shooting his mouth off about how we should be organizing an attack on 'the bastards.' Frankly, I was tired of hearing it.

Chase had made an appearance in the procession but had disappeared before we all went back to the clubhouse. He didn't seem ready yet to come back to the club. He was still licking his wounds. I didn't blame him. The man had his pride.

Aside from Cledus trying to rile up everyone about the TC, I was being pressured to pick a vice president and an enforcer. That was a problem. The enforcer's job was to protect the president's ass. There was no one better qualified for the job than me. So, guess I'd have to rely on the entire club

1

for that. As for vice president, I would have loved to appoint Colby, but I knew that was impossible. It would look suspicious and not make a shred of sense to any of the others given that he hadn't been with us very long.

Colby had come to the Banni from a smaller club called Death Proof, who got on the wrong side of the TC. Due to some lucrative drug business, the TC tried to get rid of Death Proof. Colby and a few others were taken into Banni protection and were now full-fledged members. The fact that Colby and I had secretively been lovers was neither here nor there, and, in fact, I was desperately trying to wean myself off Colby's lovin'.

It had been days since I'd pulled Colby into the woods and fucked him. He'd already told me he loved me. And yes, I loved him, too, but I couldn't say it. I wouldn't. Loving another man wasn't something the Banni would tolerate.

I'd been recruited to this club by the man I'd put down in the dirt a few days before. I'd had no choice but to take his place, although deep down I guess I knew it was my destiny all along. A promising career in the NFL was out of the question once my knees got screwed up in an underground fight. That recruiter never got to see me play. I'd had to do the fight so my mother wouldn't lose her house. After that, it was just fight after fight and lots of drugs to kill the pain.

When the leader of the Banni saved me from drug dealers I owed a fortune to, I became their enforcer. I was the one the club sent when they wanted to make someone's blood run cold when they wanted to send a clear message. There were times when I just turned off my feelings altogether. Now, the only time I felt vulnerable, the only time I felt as if someone could crush me with a single word, was when I was in Colby's arms.

It was the most wonderful yet the scariest place in the world for me. I was as addicted to Colby as I had been to painkillers. Didn't matter that either one of them could bring my life to an abrupt end. I'd finished with the drugs a long time ago, and I never thought I'd find anything harder to quit than that. But I'd been wrong. My addiction to Colby was ten times stronger than drugs.

I looked around now at the men and women in this room. They were all drunk and sad, hoisting their glasses up to the three large photographs of their fallen comrades that some of the women had hung up on the wall for the occasion. Three wasted lives, but then they'd been pretty well wasted before they'd died, as was my own.

I glanced over to see Colby sitting with Jerry and Marcel, his dog, Beauty, curled up at his feet. Pure love between those two, man and beast, not to mention the entire club who'd kinda made Beauty their mascot. Beauty was a friendly dog, trusting, and Beauty loved anyone and everyone who'd love her and feed her treats. It was nice having the dog around.

Nuts came over and sat beside me now. He placed a hand on my shoulder. "What are you doing over here by yourself?"

"Thinking," I told him.

"You going to keep me VP or what?" He passed me some nuts. The guy had earned his nickname that way.

I took a few cashews and tossed them into my mouth. "You want to be my VP?"

"Yeah," he said. "But it's your call, Boss."

"I'll take care of it tomorrow at church. Right now, I'm beat."

He nodded, standing up. "Why don't you take Tammy with you and lay down in the back?" Nuts glanced over to where Tammy sat with two of the other biker chicks. "When you going to make her legit?"

I met his gaze. "Is it a problem I want to be on my own?"

"No. But there are questions about why you don't take on an ol' lady. Only natural you have someone. Everyone does."

Great. Fucking great. "You spreading shit about me now, Nuts?" I asked, trying to hold onto my temper.

"No, man." He shook his head. "Just Tammy's been wanting to know. She wonders why you don't give it to her more often. She's been saying it's been months. You got someone else, that's cool. I know you must be getting laid somewhere, man."

Before Colby, I went out for sex, off somewhere, without the colors on my back, fucking all kinds of strangers. Tammy was my cover. I fucked her once in a while to keep the speculation about my sexuality away. Girls hung out, danced, got naked, got fucked by the guys in the club all the time. I usually tried to avoid those gangbangs. Sometimes I had no choice but to participate. It wasn't easy to get hard. Girls didn't do it for me, never had. It was just the way I was made. I'd have to focus on one of the guys and imagine I was doing him.

Poor Tammy had gotten a raw deal from me. I knew from the look on Nuts' face that the time had come for me to take her to bed again. If I didn't, there was going to be talk, some innuendos. I couldn't have that.

"It's a good idea," I told him. I needed to talk to Tammy anyway, to get her to stop complaining about the lack of attention she was getting from me. I got up and walked over to where Tammy was sitting with the girls. I knew some of the guys were watching, one of them being Colby.

Tammy looked up at me and smiled. Jesus, I hated playing the role of some Neanderthal caveman, but I was the leader now. I had to give them a show, shut them up for a while. "Hey, baby," she said.

I reached out for her and pulled her out of the chair and

up into my arms. I placed my hands on her ass, dragged her close and kissed her like there was no tomorrow. I heard the guys all catcall and cheer. Tammy put her hands in my hair. She was enjoying the kiss. I felt absolutely nothing.

The cheers and wolf whistles grew louder. I grinned at my audience, scooped Tammy up and flung her over my shoulder. I carried her off down the hallway, trying hard not to think about Colby and how he was feeling. If I'd been him, it wouldn't have been great.

I could do this. I could make love to Tammy by imagining Colby lying there in that bed. That would get me hard. And since Tammy expected hard and fast from me, that's what I gave her. There was a part of me I'd only ever shown Colby in bed, a tender, vulnerable, loving side.

Tammy fell asleep in my arms. I lay there with my eyes wide open, thinking about how I couldn't risk anyone questioning my sexuality. In spite of that fact, I felt truly ashamed. I hadn't hurt Tammy in any physical way. I'd given her exactly what she wanted, and I'd made sure she got off. I stayed hard the entire time, so it was good for her. It sucked for me. It was the price I had to pay.

Could I do this over and over? If I had to, I guess I could, but I knew I'd be putting it off, making excuses. Everyone, including this girl, was waiting for me to make it official, to declare Tammy my ol' lady but I didn't want anyone on the back of my bike, or in my bed, except Colby. It just wasn't going to be.

I eventually pulled away and left Tammy sleeping. I put on my jeans and made my way through the clubhouse. Some of the guys had passed out on the floor or on the tables. Colby wasn't among them.

The sun had just come up. I made some coffee, opened the door and stood there squinting in the sun. When I saw Beauty come running up to me, I knew Colby must still be around somewhere. I leaned down to rub the dog. Beauty flopped down so I could rub her belly.

As I did, I spotted Colby in the distance, walking up the road.

I waited until he came up on the porch.

"Early for a walk, isn't it?"

He looked at me for a second then at his dog. "Traitor," he mumbled.

"You mean me or the dog?" I met his gaze.

He shrugged. "Does it matter? Both."

I glanced behind me. "It's not the time to talk about this."

He looked down. "Let's not talk about it at all."

I felt cool hands suddenly move over my shoulder and trace over the tattoo on my back. Then arms tightened around my waist. "Hey, baby," Tammy said softly, sleepy-eyed. She kissed my shoulder, smiling at Colby. "Morning, Colby. You're up early." She took my coffee cup out of my hand and sipped some.

I could see Colby trying to smile. Only I could see the pain in his eyes when he looked at Tammy and said hello.

I wanted to touch him. I wanted to tell him that my heart was his and his alone, didn't matter that last night Tammy had had my body, didn't matter at all. I hadn't told him that, just a few weeks back, the leader of the Crushers had implied Colby might be gay. I had to make sure this kind of talk went no further, and if meant I had to make Tammy my old lady to protect Colby, I'd do it. I would have bedded the devil himself to keep Colby from harm.

Tammy nibbled my shoulder again. I tried to move away, but it would have seemed a little bizarre, so I just froze there.

Thankfully, Tammy released me. "Good coffee, baby." She swatted my butt. "Is there any more?"

"Inside," I said. "I could use a refill."

She stood on tiptoes and kissed me on the mouth, then

looked at Colby. "What about you? Want coffee, hon?"

"No," he managed. "I'm . . . ah leaving." He turned and headed off the porch. Beauty followed at his heels.

I bit my bottom lip and then bounded down the steps after him in my bare feet ignoring the rocks jabbing into my flesh. "Colby, wait!"

He reached for his helmet. He looked at me. "I'll leave Beauty here with you. I'll be back later today. Need to finish up some pool hall business."

"Don't do this," I told him.

"Don't do what?" he asked.

"Act like this. You know it had to be done."

"What part of 'I don't want to talk about this' don't you understand?" There was a flash of anger in those eyes.

I ignored him. "I have to tell you. Just last night Nuts asked me why I wasn't making Tammy my ol' lady, why I didn't fuck her more. There's been rumors about you and . . ." I sighed. "Do you think this is easy for me to do?"

He met my gaze. "I don't know. Is it?"

"Colby, please, damn it. You know the answer to that."

"I knew it was coming," he said. "I just . . . well . . . I had no idea it would hurt this bad. I went back to that tree in the woods last night, and I stayed there. That was the last time you were inside me, and I just stood there remembering and then . . . I . . ." He swallowed hard. "I told myself to accept the fact that you were inside her . . . and maybe it was the last time we would be together like that."

I reached out to touch his hand, but he withdrew it.

"Don't. Please. Listen," Colby said, "I don't blame you, Diego. I know the position you're in. Tammy is a necessary evil, but I hate her for wanting you and having you, and I have no right to hate her. I really should feel sorry for her. "

"Colby."

"I need to tell you how I feel, then we won't talk about it

anymore. It's just not fair, Diego, that because she has a vagina and I have a cock, she gets to publicly brag about having you in her bed and I don't. I never will. Every moment I've had with you, I've stolen. I can never tell anyone how much I love you. I can't put my arms around you the way she just did. I don't have the right to tell her or anyone else to keep their hands off you. Because you're not mine and I have to get it through my head that you'll never be mine."

I watched Colby get on the bike. My emotions were in turmoil. Only he could do that to me.

"So now what?" I sneered. "You run away? You run to Jerry's bed maybe?"

Colby started his bike. "Jerry? Jerry? Seriously, Diego, you jealous of Jerry? Do you really think Jerry in my bed would compensate for not having you? I thought you knew what you meant to me."

"Colby, in spite of what I have to do for the Banni, I ... I ... Well ..."

"Well, what?" he demanded. "You love me, Diego? Is that what you're trying to say?"

I swallowed and looked away.

"Doesn't matter that you can't say it. Funny thing is, baby, I know you love me. It's the only thing that kept me from losing my mind last night, the thought that even if she had you in her bed, she'd never know what it means to be truly loved by you. Only I know that. It's there when you hold me. It's there when you fuck me. And that's why you've never had to say it."

I wanted to hold onto the bike and not let go. I reached out for it, but Colby reared back and roared away.

Beauty whined in the trail of dust he left behind. I knew just how she felt.

I don't know how long I stood there before Tammy came

outside to get me. "You all right?" She handed me a full mug of coffee.

I tried to smile at her, but it suddenly hurt to smile. Everything hurt. I sipped the coffee. "Sure."

"You and Colby have a fight? He can be a little distant sometimes."

"We didn't fight," I said. I went inside, Beauty at my heel.

Tammy left to go to work at the scrapyard, and I let Nuts know I'd be calling church that afternoon around four. I needed to make sure everyone knew I was in control.

After I'd wakened Nuts out of a dead sleep to tell him about the meeting, my mom dropped by to check on the guys. Everyone felt bad about the funeral. She came toward me and almost fell over the sleeping Beauty.

She bent to scratch the dog's head. "I'm headin' to the scrapyard in a while. Beauty likes *Dr. Oz*, same as me. Today's show's all about cleavage wrinkles, and I just gotta see it before I go."

I looked at her. "You've got cleavage wrinkles?"

"No, but I like to be prepared." They curled up on the sofa together, and I went home to my little place and took a shower, changed my clothes.

I needed to get out there and ask some questions, find out who'd killed three of my members. This was the number one priority on my list. Number two was to go and see Chase, try to smooth ruffled feathers if that was even possible. Colby, well, it was best to keep my distance until things got sane again. He was hurting. So was I. Would it ever stop? Honestly? Probably not. We were bound to hurt each other over and over again as time went on.

As for Tammy, well I think before she left to go to the scrapyard, she really thought I was going to suggest something more permanent between us. She lingered for a while, waiting, with that look in her eye. Damn it, I couldn't bring myself to say anything except, "Have a nice day."

She was expecting a marriage proposal maybe. That left me cold. The last thing I wanted was marriage. I was going to put off even asking her to be my ol' lady for as long as I possibly could.

And yes, I felt like a fake, just like I'd felt making love to her, and I really wished the girl was as superficial as some of the other biker chicks. But I think Tammy had some real feelings for me, feelings I could never return no matter how hard I might pretend.

I made my rounds, asked a few people who had an ear to the ground if they had an idea about who might have attacked the Banni.

I put Tammy completely out of my mind. As for Colby, well he wasn't so easy to forget about. I carried him around in my heart, and honestly today, Colby was beginning to feel a tad heavy.

The Banni had a few friends on the force, cops we'd passed a wad of money to occasionally. I called the cell phone of one of those cops, a guy named Bradley Simpson. We'd met in a bathhouse once, had ourselves some pretty wild sex, then discovered we both wanted our sex lives to stay hidden.

When Bradley asked me to meet him outside town in a motel room, I hesitated. I was in no mood for a shakedown. The Banni hadn't paid Bradley off in three years, who knew if he'd still be a shady character or not.

As it turned out, the room was sleaze heaven, and so was Bradley. When he opened the door, I hardly recognized him. He looked like shit. Fifty pounds heavier in a dirty undershirt, and, hell, he'd lost most of his hair.

"Diego," he murmured, "heard you'd moved up in the world. Leader now? Wow. And you still look hot."

"What in hell happened to you?" I asked him, walking in

and closing the door.

"Lost my job. And . . . I got a little problem." He sniffed. "Maybe you can help me out?"

"You stink, man." I walked across the room. "Your shower broken or what?"

"Funny. Want to try it out with me? We can soap each other."

"Fuck, no," I said. "Listen, I need some info. I'll pay for it."

"Got any blow, man?" He sniffed again.

"That stuff will kill you."

"I'm half dead anyway." He flopped on the bed. "Wife found out I like cock, took the kids. Then I got fired from the force. I can't pay alimony or support payments."

"Shit," I said. "I thought my life sucked."

"Blow makes me feel alive. I'll suck your cock, anything."

I shook my head. "You sunk low, man. Shit." Damn drugs. I wondered if I'd been this pathetic years ago when I was hooked on pain pills.

"Please, Diego. We had a good time back then at the bathhouse. I still remember, man. You could fuck like a tornado, boy. Woo hoo . . . my ass still remembers it."

I sighed. This I didn't need to hear. I pointed at him. "Listen, I'll help you with your little problem, but I need to know who was behind the attack on the Banni a few weeks back. They took out three of my boys."

He wiped a hand against his nose. "I can find out."

"How long will it take?"

"A few hours. But I'll need something to tide me over, get me through."

He lay back on the bed.

I walked to the door. "Get the info."

"Diego? Anything you want."

I glanced back at him. "I'm afraid there's nothing I want

11

in this room, my friend. Get me the info, and I'll make sure you get what you need. Make some calls. I'll be back in an hour."

I got on my bike and drove to Chase's place. He lived in a log cabin in a secluded area way back in the woods about ten miles off the highway. I pushed aside all the barricades that said Keep Out and Enter at Your Own Risk and drove down the muddy road. When I pulled up in front of the cabin, I spotted his hog, so I knew he was there.

I got off the bike and removed my helmet. The first thing I noticed was the sun reflecting off the butt of a shotgun sticking about an inch out the window. "Gonna shoot me now, Chase?"

"What in fuck you want? Come to gloat?"

"No, but as far as I know, you're still a member of this club. Unless you want out? Can we talk?"

The gun slowly disappeared. I walked up onto the front porch and pulled the door open. There was Chase. One large-breasted blonde slept naked on a pullout sofa in the living room a few feet away, legs spread wide. Okay. I glanced at her and away again. "Love what you've done with the place."

"Fuck her if you want." He grunted. "She can't get enough cock, that one. Damn near wears me out, the bitch."

The cabin was one big room of squalor with an outdoor flush. Damn, how did he live like that? A sink full of dishes, everything dirty and messy, empty takeout boxes everywhere and a naked woman passed out as a centerpiece.

"She don't do the dishes, that one." Chase sneered.

I walked over, grabbed an old blanket off a chair and threw it over her. Then I grabbed a chair and sat down.

Chase leaned against the sink watching me. His face was still a mess from the fight we'd had, his eye purple, lip spilt. "I almost died, you know?" Chase told me. "They had to do some fancy stitching inside my gut thanks to you."

"You got off easy," I scoffed. "I could have killed you. Maybe I made a mistake leaving you alive."

"Maybe you did."

"That's what I was told. I refused to believe that. I have a better plan for you than a wooden box."

"You took my job."

"You didn't do it so well." I met his gaze. "Funny thing is, I never wanted it. But you know that."

"Well, you got it now, kid, so choke on it."

I stood. "I want you to be at church this afternoon."

"Why?"

"I want to make you my sergeant in arms."

Chase's eyes widened. "What the fuck? Some kind of joke, Champagne?" He scratched his beard.

"More like ironic justice. I figured after all the hits I took for you, most of it not even to do with club business, it's your turn to take a few for me."

"You need someone you can trust for that job. I'm an unlikely candidate."

I met his gaze. "If I can't trust you as my sergeant in arms, how can I trust you anywhere else in the club?"

He considered that. "You got a point. Who's gonna be VP?"

"I'm not taking that away from Nuts."

"It would have been nice to take that spot."

"Don't spit on my generosity, Chase. Sergeant in arms is the best offer you're going to get from me. I need to know you got my back, if not, well I guess I'll have to strip you of those colors."

"You'd do that? You'd spit on our history?"

"History?"

"What I've done for you. I saved your neck."

"To fill your pockets. Let's not pretend it had to do with

benevolence. What do you take me for, man?"

"Okay." He put up his hand. "I'm in." He reached for a bottle of whiskey. "Let's seal it with a drink, shall we?"

I wasn't eating or drinking anything in this place. "We'll drink to it once the club votes on it. And one more thing, if you ever double-cross me, I'll make sure you suffer for it."

Chase nodded.

"Hey . . . Diego," a silky voice cooed from under the blanket in the living room. "What'cha doing here, baby?"

"It's a little late in the day to be sleeping, isn't it, Barbie?"

"Working at the Bare Club tonight, got to get my beauty sleep. Why don't you come down? I'll dance just for you, in honor of your new job."

"I'll think about it." I looked at Chase. "The TC's new sergeant in arms has an interest in that place now. It's never been one of ours. Why is Barbie dancing there?"

"Strippers don't like the manager at our place."

I looked at Barbie. "Is that why you aren't dancing at Jugs anymore? The Banni own most of the place."

"The guy running the place is mean, honey," she muttered. "He doesn't pay, and he's always making us suck him off."

"And you knew that?" I looked at Chase.

"That's why I told her to change jobs."

"Freddie is supposed to oversee the club. Is he blinded by pussy? He's not doing his job. Who's managing it?"

"A freak called Niles," Barbie hollered. She wrapped the blanket around her and came over to the table. She rubbed my arm and smiled at me. "Freddie don't listen when we girls talk."

"I'm listening," I told her. "This stuff true, about him not paying and making you girls blow him?"

She nodded. "Yeah, he's a bastard."

"I'll have a word with him. The Bare Club's not our territory. We can't protect you there."

"That patch looks good on you, baby." She traced the word President with her finger. "You take on an ol' lady yet? I wouldn't mind."

"Get in the shower," Chase snapped.

Barbie winked at me and scurried off.

"I'll talk to this Niles guy later today," I told Chase. "Send Barbie back to Jugs."

"I will."

"And I want you looking after Jugs from now on. Listen when the girls speak, okay?"

"Okay."

"So I'll see you this afternoon at four?"

"I'll be there."

"Right now, I need you to call a couple of the guys and head out to a motel on the highway."

"To do what exactly?"

"To do something you once did for me years ago. And you're not to leave until the job is done."

I drove back to the hotel to visit with my washed-up cop. By the time I was ready to leave the motel I had a name. Teresa's half-brother, Purnell Torrens, fresh out of the pen. Along with a few of his redneck buddies, they thought they had a claim on the drugs.

I dialed Badger's personal cell phone.

"Diego?" he said. "What's going on, brother?"

Brother? Okay. "Teresa's half-brother, a guy named Purnell Torrens." Teresa. Man, would we never be rid of her? She was dead but was still causing grief. She had started all the gang problems, first by trying to kill Jerry, Colby's best friend and former leader of Death Proof. She'd put him in the hospital for weeks. Then she put a bounty on Colby.

Turned out she was running a drug empire out of her cute little tomato farm. She had so many games goin' on, and she'd been bangin' Franklin, which led to his death, and she'd been bangin' Chase, too.

According to Bradley, Purnell Torrens and his buddies were responsible for the attack on our clubhouse the other night. Not out of brotherly affection, I was sure, but because they wanted in on the drugs. The TCs were running that stuff. Drugs weren't our scene.

"I figure they'll try the same shit on the TC soon enough," I told Badger. "You want to show these bastards a united front on this one?"

"You name the time and place. I'll be there with my members. You got an address?"

"I will get the lowdown on their routine, then call you when the time is right."

"We'll be ready." He hung up.

As I walked to the door, Bradley called out to me again, "Diego?"

I turned and looked at him.

"There's something I didn't tell you."

"What's that?"

Bradley began to tell me about Torrens while up in the pen, then he said, "He made a friend when he was there, someone you know."

It took me a minute to recover after he said the name. Memories flashed through my head, none of them good. "So?" I managed.

"Lafleur got out on parole last week. Word is, he's biding his time. Watch your back, man."

I hardly had time to digest that when Bradley said, "I kept my part. Where's the blow?"

I glanced at him. "In a few minutes, some pretty tough Banni are going to walk into this room and do you the favor of your life."

"They're going to bring me some blow?"

"No. They're going to dry you out."

I walked outside and shut the door. I could hear the drone of the bikes coming in my direction. Chase was leading the pack. He'd taken his first order from me as his leader. So far, so good.

I stopped by the scrapyard on the way to the club. Tammy came out from behind the desk and kissed me the moment I walked in. This wasn't going away. My mother was behind the desk. Her eyes widened a little, but she didn't say anything.

The phone rang, and Tammy hurried to answer it. I walked over to where my mother stood. She was sorting through some bills. "Hello, big shot," she said.

I grinned. "Hey, Mama."

"You still look like a little boy when you smile like that." She came out from behind the counter and took my arm. We walked outside. "What's with all that lovey-dovey shit between you and Tammy? You sleep with her again?"

I shrugged.

"You're going to hurt that girl something awful, Diego. Why you want to do that to her, break her heart like that?"

"I don't want to. It's complicated." I glanced around the scrapyard.

"Something to prove again, I suppose? Got to prove you're a man? I can see that."

"I didn't come to talk about me and Tammy. I came to see how you were."

"Tired."

"Why don't you go home and rest?"

"And do what, dwell on the fact I'm tired?"

"Have you spoken to the doctor yet? What did he say?"

"Doctors." She clicked her tongue. "They don't know a damn thing. Except Dr. Oz."

"Mama?" I looked at her. "Tell me what he said."

17

"Says I might have some kind of tumor or something . . . you know down there where it's useless now."

My heart sank. "Tumor?" I met her gaze. "Why in the hell didn't you tell me?"

"My little boy got enough to worry about, and now this Tammy thing."

"Never mind Tammy. I'll handle it. Did they do a test? Is it . . . cancer?"

"They don't know. They won't know until they do some biopic thing."

"Biopsy?"

"Yeah." She hugged my arm. "You seen Colby since this morning? That boy looked very down when I saw him an hour ago. He's at the clubhouse. Talk to him, son."

I sighed. "I talk to him all the time, Mama."

"You know what I mean."

"There's nothing to say. Now, I'm taking you home."

She shook her head. "Feels better to be here. Tammy is a good girl. She takes over when I need a break. It occupies my mind."

"Okay. You call me if you want to go home. Someone will take you."

"Colby said he would take me. He gave me his cell phone."

"Okay." I kissed her and got back on my bike, realizing I didn't say goodbye to Tammy.

Colby was sitting outside the clubhouse with about six other members when I drove up. When he saw me, he walked inside. Great. I'd planned to take him down to Jugs with me. I knew Colby wouldn't get all distracted by the naked women like the other guys did. I needed to have a word with this Niles guy. The Banni owned sixty percent interest in that club, and I didn't need this guy scaring the girls off.

I made small talk with some of the members, patted Beauty a few times, then went to find Colby. Beauty walked at my heels.

Colby was in the back room where we held church. He was slumped in one of chairs. He looked up when he saw me, then called to Beauty. "Ought to know Beauty would be following you around. Church already?"

"No." I checked my watch. "In two hours. I need you to come with me now."

"Okay." He stood. "Where we going?"

"Jugs."

"Ooh," he teased, "I'm so excited."

"Very cute." I grimaced.

"What's up?"

"The manager is an octopus, mauling the girls and holding on to their paychecks. I need to set him straight."

"It sounds like someone hasn't been taking care of business."

"Exactly." I called to Nuts on the way out. "We're going to be at Jugs. Make sure people are assembled for when I get back."

He gave me a little salute.

"Take care of Beauty," Colby called out, and we made for our bikes.

Nuts took Beauty inside.

Colby followed me to Bennington Avenue and parked his bike in the parking lot behind Jugs. It was a small but popular strip joint, quite legit and considered to be on the upscale side, all glass and colored lights.

Colby took off his helmet and got off his bike, while I returned a call from Chase concerning Bradley.

"We put him in an ice-cold bath," Chase said. "The guy was pissed. Cursing your name just like you did me, kid."

"Well stay with him until three thirty, then leave a couple of prospects to guard him. I need you at church."

"I hear you."

Colby was waiting for me. I got off my bike and indicated the back entrance. "You bring me along 'cause I like cock and won't get distracted?" he asked me.

"Precisely."

"All the time I thought you liked me." He gave me an impish grin.

"That too," I said.

We walked in, avoiding the main room where some sultry music was blaring and proceeded down a carpeted hallway. A client walked out of the bathroom and froze when he saw us.

"It's okay," I said. "Keep walking."

The man hurried back to the main room, and we turned the corner.

Colby chuckled.

The office was beside the girls' dressing room. There was another exit that led into the main part of the club where the girls danced. A young woman walked out of the dressing room. I recognized her from the club parties. I think her name was Shirley.

"Oh, Diego . . ." the tall brunette purred as she walked by me in a silk dressing robe. "You're a walking wet dream."

I just grinned, then heard her say, "Ooh and, Colby, you're sooo cute."

I glanced back over my shoulder just in time to see her reach out and pinch Colby's cheek before continuing on her way.

"Why are you a walking wet dream and I'm . . . sooo cute?" He imitated Shirley's intonation and rubbed his face.

I laughed. "You are sooo cute." I mocked, trying to pinch his cheek again. He pushed my hand away, but he was smiling.

A little man in his forties wearing glasses poked his head

out of the office just ahead. "Can I help you?"

"Niles!" I exclaimed.

He nodded. "Yes."

"Chase isn't the leader of the Banni anymore, so I thought it was time I came to introduce myself."

"You're ah . . . oh, you're Diego Champagne."

The guy had the good sense to look scared when he said it.

"Not to mention a walking wet dream," Colby sniggered behind me.

I held back a smile. "That's right, and I've had some complaints about you. Have you been a naughty boy, Niles?"

"No, I . . . Who told you . . . who complained? Was it the bitches?"

"First of all, you don't get anywhere by calling the girls bitches. You also don't get anywhere by putting your hands all over them without getting a personal invitation."

"They're all whores."

"Um, which makes you the whoremaster?"

He shook his head. "You know."

"Not really. From now on, no means no, unless you want to find a new job. Okay?"

He nodded.

"And just what's going on with the payroll? Seems some women aren't getting paid. You're not stealing from them, are you? Because it means you're stealing from the Banni."

"If they don't bring in the customers, they don't get paid. I've warned them to play up to the clients. I've never stolen a cent from the club." He took a step back as I walked into his office.

"You know," I picked a paperweight off his desk and studied it. "I think you're a liar and I don't like you." I met his gaze.

He backed up again. "Why? I'm a nice guy. I'm not a liar."

I turned to Colby. "Do you like this guy?"

"No," Colby said, shaking his head. "I don't like him."

"Would you mind if he wasn't around?"

"I could live with that." Colby folded his arms across his chest.

"Close the door," I told Colby.

"Now look, listen, Diego, Mr. Champagne, Sir, I . . . I'll be better. I'll be good. I'll do whatever you want. I'll be nice. I won't touch them."

The door closed. I could feel Colby at my shoulder.

I looked down at Niles. "Then I want you to repeat after me. 'I won't fondle the girls anymore.'"

"I won't fondle them anymore."

"I will pay them every week for every hour they work."

"I will . . . I will pay them every cent . . . every week. I promise."

"I won't be mean to them. I'll be respectful and never call them bitches again."

"Yeah . . . yeah . . . that, all that."

"Say it," I insisted, pushing him to his knees in front of me. He'd broken out in a sweat and was shaking all over. I almost felt sorry for him.

"I . . . won't be mean and call them bitches, and I'll pay and I'll . . . I won't touch them or . . . slap their butts or make them suck anything they don't want to suck."

"What a good boy." I patted his head. "Now get up and be a manager. Be a good manager and good things will come to you."

"Yes, sir. I will. I promise."

Colby opened the door.

I walked out.

"See ya," Colby told the man and followed me down the hallway and outside. Colby suddenly started to laugh.

I raised an eyebrow.

"You're so macho." He nudged me. "You make my dick so hard."

I laughed. "Stop flirting with me."

He sobered. "Okay."

"Colby," I said as we put on our helmets, "thanks for coming with me. I mean it."

"Did you talk to your mom today?" he asked.

"She's sick."

"I know."

"You know? How do you know?"

"She told me earlier. She's going to be all right. She's tough like you."

I got on my bike. "Stubborn like me, you mean."

"Diego?"

"What?"

"You know I'll be there. I'll be there for both of you when you need me."

"I know that." I didn't tell him what was really bothering me deep down. There was too much going on to tell him about Lafleur.

"And one more thing," Colby said.

I looked over at him.

"You really are a walking wet dream."

I laughed. "And you, you're sooo cute. I just wanna pinch your little cheeks."

"Which ones?" he deadpanned. "Face or ass?"

We were both laughing as we took off on our bikes and headed back to the clubhouse.

Chapter Two

A s I sat in the president's chair for the first time, I glanced around the table. All full-patched members in our chapter were present. When Chase walked in, everyone stared.

Colby sat beside Jerry, a couple of chairs away from a brooding Cledus.

I brought down the hammer and declared the meeting open. I got right to work. "I need to make some changes as leader, but these changes need to be voted on so there will be several votes taken today. I want these issues resolved quickly because we have more pressing matters to take care of."

Everyone knew I was talking about the recent attack on our club.

"I've decided that Nuts will stay on as V.P. Is there any objections to that?"

No one said anything, so I said, "Carried." I took a breath. The next one would be controversial. "I asked Chase to be sergeant in arms."

The room exploded at that point into an unintelligible shouting match. The loudest protestor was Colby, who got to his feet and shouted, "Hell, no."

I called for silence. I looked at Colby. "Say what you have to."

"The sergeant in arms needs to be one hundred percent loyal to the leader. I don't trust Chase. I don't think anyone in this room trusts Chase to protect you." Colby looked at Chase. "You ready to give your life for Diego?"

Chase stood. "I am loyal to this club. The Banni is my life. You are all my brothers." He looked at me. "Diego is my leader. I will lay down my life for him in spite of our differences."

I looked at Colby. "Anything else?"

He sat down, arms crossed. He'd made his opinion known. The motion passed by a slim margin. I moved on. I glanced at Colby. "I'd like to make Colby road captain."

There was some applause, some sneers.

I put up my hand. "Colby knows the roads, he knows bikes. He is organized and will be good for mapping out the track, and the refueling stops." I glanced at him. "Interested?"

He nodded. "Yeah. Anything you want."

"Let's vote." I knew there were no strong feelings one way or another. The road captain rode up front with the leader. I guess it was, in part, selfish. I couldn't fuck him, but at least we could ride together. It was the next best thing.

The vote passed quickly, and I was onto other business. I wanted better record keeping. I doubled up on the treasurer and the bookkeeping. I appointed different teams to oversee the clubs and keep track of our friends on the outside.

I left the most contentious for last. "I know who attacked us the other night."

The room got loud.

I put up my hand. "Wait. Listen. I've enlisted the TC's help in this."

Again, the room erupted. Chase was the most irate. "You did what?" He was on his feet. "Is this your first act as our fearless leader, to kowtow to the fucking Crushers?"

"I'm not kowtowing to anyone." I stood and stared everyone down. The room got quiet. "We are partners in the drug trade with the TC. We both own a piece of a very profitable business."

"We own it," Chase muttered.

"Yeah." I looked at him. "But it's on TC territory. You think it will be free to cross that line?"

He looked down at the table.

"More importantly, right now there is someone else out there who thinks they should own a piece, too. We have a mutual enemy. They attacked us, and it's only a matter of time until they strike the TC. There are times we have to come together for the good of both clubs, and this is one of them."

Again, there was a heated discussion. I was growing weary. I slammed down the hammer, then threw it across the room. It hit the door. Everyone stopped talking. "We don't have to have war all the time, do we? When it makes sense to join forces, we need to put past grudges behind us and work together. Have your say, one at a time. Then we'll put it to a vote." I gave everyone their chance.

Members brought up past gripes with the TC, which again I reminded them of the alternative. Thankfully several saw my point of view, including Colby, who echoed what I said. "Diego is right. We can't always be killing each other. We're stronger together than apart. I think we should work together when we have common interests. It just makes sense."

"Listen to you." Colby's father laughed. "Just a punk, not around in the old days when the TC was shooting us down like dogs before the big, tough Banni rose up to protect us. They wiped out our club, and now you want to kiss their asses? You know fuck all, Colby, about nothing."

Colby sprang up. "We can't all live in the past like you, old man."

That was it. They were out of their seats. Colby moved so fast none of us could stop him. He was on top of his father, hands around his throat. It took several members to pull him off.

"Take Colby outside," I said, "and cool him off."

Colby walked out on his own.

Cledus was on the floor, clutching his throat. I walked over to him. "You spoke out of turn."

"Fuck you." He spat on the floor.

"If you want out, say so. Do it before I put you out."

Cledus looked up at me. "Then do it, put me out. You'll regret it. Just because you're big and tough doesn't mean that one day someone won't put you down like a dog."

"That sounds like a threat." I reached down and pulled him up by the front of his vest. I could feel some of the others move back. I dragged Cledus out the door of the room and into the main hall. He fought me all the way.

Colby was sitting there on a chair with two of the other guys. When he saw me with Cledus, he didn't make a move, just watched.

I yanked off Cledus's jacket, then tore off his patch. I threw the jacket back at him. "Consider yourself without a club. If you want to kill TC, go for it. Now, get out of my sight before I decide to burn that Death Proof tattoo off your back with a blow torch."

"You don't have a right."

I dragged him off the floor and pulled him up to my chest. "Tell me again what I have a right to do. You were given our protection, given a home when you lost yours, and this is how you repay that debt?"

I could see the sweat rolling down his forehead. "There was a time when I could have taken you, Champagne."

"Yeah, well, old man, that time has passed, unless you still want to try?" I met his gaze and waited.

The others stood still. I looked at Colby. He looked away. It was a signal to do what I wanted. I didn't want to kill Colby's old man. In spite of the fact that there was a lot of bad blood between them, they were still family. "I want you gone." I released him and turned away. I knew he was going to attack me. It was time to test out Chase's loyalty.

I took two steps and saw Chase grab Cledus from behind. I turned and landed Cledus a good punch to the face. A knife fell out of his hand to the floor. The punch knocked him out cold. "Get him out of here."

I watched two of my guys carry Cledus out the door. I turned to the rest. "We'll consider the meeting adjourned but stick around. We're going to be on the move soon." I looked at Marcel and Freddie. "I need you guys to do something for me. Come on."

I gave Marcel and Freddie the address of Teresa's half-brother. "Now, only you guys are to know about this for now. I want you to watch the place. Don't let anyone see you and don't make a move until I say so. You're to call me the minute you spot someone going in or out. I want to know their every move. Is that clear?"

They both nodded and took off. I went back into the conference room and sank into my chair.

Colby knocked on the door. "Yeah?" I looked at him.

"I'm sorry for the trouble."

"No trouble. It was time I got rid of him. Are you okay with that?"

He nodded, came in and closed the door. "Yeah but there's something I'm not okay with. Why didn't you make me sergeant in arms?"

The question surprised me. "You know why. There would have been opposition. You're too young and . . ."

"I would have taken a bullet for you." He met my gaze. He lowered his voice. "I would die for you."

I swallowed.

He touched my arm. He looked down into my eyes. "Thanks for the road captain though."

"I needed to make one of the former death proof members an officer, really integrate you."

"That's not the only reason." He smiled faintly.

"No, it's not the only reason," I replied.

There was a knock on the door. Colby moved away from me. He said hello as Chase walked in and left us alone.

"You okay?" Chase asked.

"Fine. Thanks for that out there."

"I recognize a test when I see one. You knew he would do that. You could have protected yourself."

"Yes."

"So, I passed?"

"You passed." I stood and laid a hand on his shoulder. "I'm going to take a little nap in the back room for a while."

"I'm going to check on our boy at the motel," Chase said.

"Keep me posted," I told him and headed to the back room.

I was tired, and I knew what was in store for later. I needed to be well rested.

I fell into an uneasy sleep and was seized by a dream, one of the dirtiest dreams I'd ever had, and it starred Colby. It was so real, I thought he was there with me in that room.

What are you doing? We could be caught.

Makes it so much more exciting, doesn't it? You're exciting. I want it. I want you.

Colby stood a few feet away. He was completely naked and hard. He was touching himself all over, and he was mine. "Come to me," I whispered. "Come here, baby. Let me help you with that."

He smiled and crawled on the bed between my open thighs. I felt trembling fingers unzipping my pants. I couldn't wait for him to touch it, to take my cock into his mouth. I reached out and felt nothing but air, yet I was sure that my cock was trapped in his velvet mouth, being bathed by his sensational tongue, and surrounded by his soft yet determined lips.

"Oh God," I moaned. "God, yes . . . yes. Fuck!"

Then as I was coming, I saw his face. He sat astride me. "My own personal Harley," he teased. "So hard, always ready and . . . baby, I love you. Don't you know that? I love you so much." I was inside him, pumping up into the air, into . . . nothing. My eyes flew open. I was alone in the dark. No Colby. I sat up in bed. I knew someone was in the room with me. Guys like me never really sleep.

When I could focus, I saw Tammy standing there at the foot of the bed. I was so disappointed it wasn't Colby. If I had been capable, I would have broken down and cried.

"Diego?"

The voice was soft and feminine not husky and deep, and it left a bad taste.

"What are you doing in here?" I snapped, then instantly regretted my temper. I looked down to check if my pants were zipped up, then I lifted my legs off the bed and planted them on the floor.

"I missed you," she said.

Words of love meant to make someone smile only served to irritate me. "Shouldn't you be working?" I raked my hands through my hair as I sat there on the side of the bed trying to shake that dream. Damn. Had I called out Colby's name? It had seemed so real.

She sat down beside me. "What's up with us? The girls want to know if they should be throwing us a party or something."

I stood up almost at once. I didn't want anyone touching me right now. "A party for what?"

"You know," she said.

Then I realized what she meant, a party to declare us a couple or engaged or . . . damn it. "I'm too busy for that now." It sounded callous. It was callous. I felt like a shit. If I could have been honest, I would have. But I needed Tammy right now to make everything seem as it should be.

"Baby? Who were you dreaming about?"

"Why?" I turned to look at her sitting there. "What did you hear? What are you doing anyway sneaking around like that? I was trying to grab some sleep."

"I wasn't sneaking around," she said. She looked frightened.

I didn't want to make her afraid of me. I sometimes forget who I am, forget I'm supposed to be someone to fear. I softened my tone and sat down beside her again. "It's okay. I'm not mad."

"Whoever it was . . . you . . . must be crazy about her." She searched my face, then stroked my cheek. "I know it wasn't me you were making love to."

I kissed her forehead. "It was a just a dream."

A knock sounded on the door just as she hugged me. I looked up to see Colby standing there, and I separated myself from Tammy. Colby took one look at her and mumbled, "Sorry, I'll come back."

"No." Tammy stood. "You two got business." She leaned down and kissed me on the mouth. "We'll talk later, baby." She hurried out, and Colby looked at me.

"What is it?" I sighed and looked at the floor.

He held out my cell phone. "You left it in the conference room. Thought you might need it. I didn't intend to disturb you, was just going to . . ."

Colby was rambling. I knew why he was talking for the sake of it. We both did. I walked over, pushed the door shut with my foot and took my phone. As I did, I pushed him back against the wall and stole a rough kiss.

He clung to me, one hand moving down my flank, then slipping over to the zipper on my jeans. "Jesus," he groaned against my mouth, "you're already hard." He pushed me away. "Wonder why."

"Seriously?" I eyed him, my chest heaving. "Tammy had nothing to do with it."

"You sure? What was it like to fuck her?"

The truth was, I didn't remember, and yet I could remember every detail about the last time I'd fucked him.

"I was dreaming just now." I closed my eyes a moment. "I was dreaming about fucking you." I opened my eyes and looked at him. "If I could stop, I would."

Colby dragged my mouth back to his and then reared back. "You were dreaming about me and embracing her."

"Damn it," I pleaded. "You know I have no choice."

He nodded. "Doesn't make it easier." He stared at me hard for a minute, then kissed me again.

"We can't." My protest was muffled by his kisses.

"Just let me . . ." Colby struggled with my zipper. "Touch it, feel it." Seconds later he had my cock out of my pants and was squeezing it gently in his fist.

My knees were like rubber as he swung me around against the closed door. He continued to stroke me, and I closed my eyes as he jerked me to release.

I stifled my cry against his shoulder, then felt his cock nudge my thigh. He grabbed my hand and guided it to his open fly, pressing it against his erection. When I ran my fingers over the tip, he trembled all over. "God help me, Diego." He lowered his head against my chest as I moved my tightened fist over his shaft. "Fuck, Fuck," he groaned. "I only want you, just you, and that's not fair."

No. It wasn't fair, but the way I felt about him wasn't either. I felt his semen run through my fingers now as Colby let out a gasp of breath. He turned and pressed his ass into my groin, and I closed my eyes. "Don't do this to me," I groaned as I let my head bang back against the door.

"Imagine you're fucking me," Colby whispered. "Move your hips . . . just the way you do when you're inside me."

I placed my hands on his hips and went through the motions, but it only aggravated my appetite to be inside him for real. Damn it, had it really come to this? "You're going to drive me out of my mind," I grunted as he kept encouraging me to move.

Colby grabbed my hand and placed it back on his cock. He was hard again. So was I. I had to have him. All rationale was gone. I pushed his jeans down and slid my cock against his crack. Colby urged me on. "Yes."

"It's going to hurt like hell. I have no lube, no condom."

"It hurts worse without you there. Damn it, Diego. It's killing me, having you around me and not being able to touch you."

My cock was still slick with its own juices. "I don't want to hurt you."

"I don't care," he grunted. "Do it."

The knocking at the door almost gave me a heart attack.

"Diego, you in there?"

We both scrambled to do up our pants. My heart was pounding like a drum. When it was safe to open the door, I tried to look as normal as possible. It was a performance worthy of an academy award.

Marcel stood in the doorframe.

"Came to give him his phone," Colby told Marcel unnecessarily after I said hello.

"Tried to call you," Marcel said to me. "We got Torrens and his buddies all in one place. Looks like they're settling in for the night and having a big party, saw a lot of chicks, stripper types with big knockers, and crates of beer being carted in."

"Guess we'll have to get ourselves invited," I said.

"So, tonight is the night to strike while they're all in one place then?"

"You got it," I said. "Where's Freddie?" I left the room.

"He's still watching them."

"Good, go back there and wait there for us. Don't do anything, just watch."

He nodded. "Okay."

"Colby," I said, "get hold of everyone. I want them all here by nine tonight."

"Where are you going?" He called as I walked to the door.

"I need to check on something, then talk to Badger."

"You want me to come with you?"

"No. It's better if I go alone."

Colby was on the phone. I drove back to the motel. Chase was sitting outside smoking a cigarette. I got off my bike and asked him how our friend was.

"Pissed," Chase said. "Nuts is with him."

"I want four prospects and a couple of wannabes watching him tonight. Make sure the hotel room is paid up, tell them you don't want maid service and keep him in there."

"I've got all that covered."

"I'm going to need you and Nuts back at the clubhouse."

"You found them?"

I nodded. "Freddie and Marcel are watching them. They're all there, getting ready for a party."

Chase smirked. "We'll show 'em a party they won't forget. We don't need the Crushers, we can do this."

"We need to show the Crushers we are both under threat, show a united front to these guys. Who knows who else they're working with?"

Chase walked me to the bike. "What do you mean? You know something I don't, don't you, Diego? I know that look."

"Well . . ." I took a breath. "Word is that when Torrens was up in the pen, he was in the same cell block as some of the Boys."

"As in The Boys of Baton Rouge?"

I nodded.

"Thought that gang was finished, after all those arrests ten years back."

"There's still a few bad elements around, like Lafleur."

Chase's mouth hung open. He would remember Gilles better than anyone. "The Gilles Lafleur, the one you—"

I put up a hand. "Yeah. Apparently, he and Torrens got to be real good buddies in the joint. I'm sure Torrens told him about the drugs, and maybe my name came up. I really didn't think Torrens would go up against us or the Crushers unless he had some serious heavyweight in the background. Lafleur is an entity all his own."

"Yeah, and my bet is he still hates your guts. He lost his seat as president because of you."

I nodded. "See you at nine."

Lafleur and I had some history, history that had me deep in thought when my cell phone rang. I'd been waiting on a call back from Badger, to find out if he was going to have some of his boys there tonight, so I was surprised when I saw it was my mom. "Hey, Mama." I straddled the bike. "It's really not the time."

"Well, you'll have to make time there, Mr. Busy Man, or Mr. President now, whatever you're called. I've got to go into the hospital."

My hand tightened on the phone. "When?"

"Tomorrow morning. They don't like that thing inside me. I guess they want to cut it on out, but I got a whole slew of stuff they wanna do first."

"Shit. Okay. I'll be there to take you. What time?"

"You don't need to take me anywhere. I just want someone to look out for my house, maybe one of your little grunts could drive by once in a while? And if I don't come out of there, I've signed papers to—"

"Mama, it's not going to happen. I'll take care of it." I waited. "Are you all right?"

"Of course."

"You want me to drop by?"

"I hear you're going to war. You got no time for visiting."

Jesus. How does she know these things?

"'War? Now, where did you hear that?"

"I hear things. I'm not deaf. I know you boys are going to retaliate for what happened to Dave, Jackson, and Giles. I know how things work. I've been watching you for long enough. You may not even be alive tomorrow, child."

"Mama," I protested.

"Be careful." She was sniffing. "If you're still alive tomorrow, I have to be there at seven."

"I'll be there," I assured her. "And stop crying."

She hung up.

Two minutes later, she called back again.

"Yeah?"

"I love you," she said. "Didn't want anything to happen to either one of us without you knowing that."

"I know that," I told her. "And nothing is going to happen. I love you back."

"Child," she muttered, "that's a given. Don't think I don't know, and that love is the most precious thing. That's why don't you let no one take that from me." She hung up again.

I sat there and stared at the phone. When it rang again, it was the call I'd been waiting for. I explained the situation to Badger. "We'll be there. I'll bring ten, that enough?"

"More than enough."

He hung up.

I tucked my phone back in my pocket and threw my helmet in the back. I drove for a while, letting the wind blow through my hair. I circled back to my mom's house. Colby's bike was parked out front. It was nice of him to take such an interest in my mother.

My mother opened the door when she heard my bike. I walked up on the porch, and she hugged me. It had more to do with tonight than what she had to face tomorrow. I knew that. My hug back was all about her though. It had always been about her. She was all I'd had from the first moment I could remember. She'd always been there for me. I couldn't stand the thought that one day she wouldn't be.

Colby's dog was barking, and I realized she expected her due. I broke away from Mama and petted her, then I looked up at Colby.

My mother looked at me, then at Colby and smiled. "You're a good fit," she said softly. "Although you gotta watch this boy's temper," she told Colby, referring to me.

I didn't expect that. I just looked down at the floor a minute.

My mother kicked me in the shin.

"Ouch," I said. "What did you do that for?"

"Say something, stupid. Colby and I been talking." She walked over and hugged Colby. "I think I've adopted him. He's far too cute to be busting heads."

Colby blushed. Then he laughed and hugged my mother back.

"I'm cute," I teased.

"No." Colby shook his head. "You're . . ." He stopped. "My coffee's cold." He walked into the kitchen.

Mama looked at me. "That boy loves you."

"Mama, don't go getting crazy. You know this has to stay between us. The club would never . . ."

"To hell with the club a minute. I know you're not being true to yourself." She pointed at me. "I know you're not this person." She waved her hand over me as if wanting to transform me into something else. "You look the role, and you play the part so damn good, Diego. But you're there cause of me, me and your no-good daddy. That's the only reason." There were tears running down her face.

"I can't stay."

"He's not going to stay," my Mama said as Colby reappeared. "I'm feeding him truth. My boy don't like that. He won't listen."

"Mama, stop it," I told her. "I came to see if you were okay and to tell you that I'll be here tomorrow."

She nodded and looked at Colby. "Love put him in that vest, you know that?"

Colby nodded silently.

"Ask him about it," she said. "Maybe he'll tell you. And I know something else. Only love will pull him out of that vest, too." She looked at me. "And this time it's not a child's love for his mama that's going to do that. You're a man now. The love is of a different kind."

I just looked at her. This was too much even for me. Especially now I knew that Lafleur was out there somewhere and had joined forces with Teresa's family. "I have to go," I said again. I headed for the door.

I was almost to my bike when Colby caught my arm. "If you don't want me here, tell me."

I turned and looked at him. "I never said that. She likes you. I'm grateful you—" I stopped.

"She's right you know." Colby met my gaze.

"She doesn't understand," I told him. "I can't get out. Is that what you're asking me to do?"

"No. I mean ... I don't know anymore." He sighed. "I look at my father, wasted life, no good to anyone ... and I wonder if he hadn't been in Death Proof, what would I be? Where would I be? There's got to be something better than this."

I just shook my head.

"It's such a relief to be here with your mother. Do you know why?"

I waited for his answer.

"She's part of you. She knows how much I love you. I can say it over and over to her, and it's all right. I can shout it at the top of my lungs, and it feels so right to do that. And she loves you, too, so we have a bond. It's like she's the mother I always wanted."

I leaned over and hugged him. I didn't know what else to do. I just hugged him. When I released him, Colby said, "The first time I ever thought of the possibility of getting out and making a life with you, the two of us together, not hiding from anyone, walking down the street holding your hand, telling everyone you're mine, was when I saw that fear in your mother's eyes. I'd never thought about that before your mother gave me this dream, Diego."

I swallowed. "That's all it is, a dream," I told him. I couldn't build up his hopes for something that would never happen. "You shouldn't let her fill your head with nonsense," I said. "This isn't a Disney film."

He reached out and grabbed my arm. "Why is it nonsense?"

"I have too much right now to think about, Colby. I can't engage in fantasy."

"Talk to me."

"You don't want to know."

"Yes, yes, I do want to know. Is it tonight? Are you worried about—"

"No. The TC will be there with us. There's nothing to worry about. There are some things you don't know, things I never told you."

"Like what? Tell me now. I'm listening."

"I had a chance to be a pro football player. That's all I ever wanted to do, play football, and I was good at it. But before a big-time recruiter got to see me play, the bank tried to take my mother's house away because she was a woman and because she was a person of color. I was working for a guy who was managing extreme fights at that time. I went to him and begged him for a fight that weekend so I could pay the bank on Monday. The fight was two days before the game where I could have been chosen as a draft choice for the NFL."

Colby moved closer. "What happened?"

"I did the fight. I was pretty battered, and I never made the game and I . . . well my knees were damaged. I used to be able to run like the wind. Those days were over after that."

"Oh, Diego, I'm sorry, baby. I didn't know."

I shrugged. "I got hooked on painkillers after that. I did fight after fight, and I won every one, but I'd suffer from the injuries for days. I got a lot of attention, especially from biker clubs. The Banni rescued me from the drug dealers. I was so in debt, they were going to kill me. Chase dried me out and made me sergeant in arms."

"But you've paid your debt fifty times now."

"Do you think it's easy to just walk away, Colby? Look at me, I'm president of this club."

"Anything worth having is never easy. What made you tell me that now? Why not before?"

"The guy I fought in that fight was the leader of the Baton Rouge Boys. You know who they are?"

"They were a biker club, quite ruthless, but they're gone now, aren't they?"

"Mostly, but Gilles Lafleur just got out of the joint."

Colby narrowed his eyes. "The former leader?"

"I got the fight because Lafleur thought he could take me.

I fucked him up as good as he did me. He destroyed my chances of ever playing pro ball, and I blinded him in one eye."

"My God."

"Yeah, and worse, his presidency was challenged, and he lost his patch because of that fight."

Colby took a breath.

"Teresa's half-brother was in prison with Gilles Lafleur. They've joined forces."

Colby looked stunned. "He wants revenge."

"Lafleur swore that one day he'd kill me for what I'd done to him. He wasn't joking. I was hoping he'd never get out of there."

"You need to tell the others."

"No. I will deal with Lafleur on my own. He's mine. He took everything from me that night. He smashed my knee-caps with a metal pipe. That's the only reason he isn't dead, but now that he's out, I'm going to kill him."

Colby shook his head. He wound his arms around me and held me for a moment. "No. Please, don't. You're really scaring me now. Diego, I still won't give up on that dream your mother put in my head. I don't care what you say. If you really love me, one day we'll ride out of here together. We'll take your mom, the dog, and we'll go, and we'll never look back." He quickly kissed my cheek and backed away.

I smiled at him. It was a beautiful dream. "It's not because I don't love you," I told him softly. I sucked in some breath as Colby's eyes widened. He waited for the words, words I'd held back for so long. I had to say them now, and I knew it. If I didn't, with Lafleur out of the joint, I might not get the chance. "I do," I whispered. "I really do love you, Colby, and I will love you until my very last breath." I got on my bike, pushed down on the gas before he could say anything, and roared out onto the road.

Nine o'clock sharp and both clubs had surrounded the house booming with loud music. When we all drove up in front the house, twenty-five screaming motorcycles engines, it got the occupants' attention. I got off my bike at the same time Badger did. The others followed.

I kicked open the door. Badger walked over and killed the music. Everyone froze, but I knew the ones we really wanted hadn't stuck around. They were scrambling for weapons. I directed my boys to do a sweep of the house. I glanced at the terrified party guests. "I'm really disappointed," I said. Looks like our invitations got lost in the mail."

"Unless," Badger said with a grin, "we weren't invited."

"Now that would be just plain rude," I said. I walked into the living room and pointed out the girls. "Ladies, unless you'd like to party with the big boys, I suggest you scurry on home."

The girls quickly filed out. When they got to the street past the bikes, they began to run.

Badger walked over to the men in the room telling them to stay put. A few of our guys brought down three men from upstairs a few minutes later. I was disappointed to see that Lafleur was not among them.

"Now," I said, looking from one to another, "which one of you is Torrens?"

Two of the other guys pointed to the guy in the middle.

"Fuckers," he muttered.

I laughed.

"I'm not dying for you, man," one of them yelled.

"Badger, do you mind if we escort these fine gentlemen back to our clubhouse for a little . . . interrogation? You're welcome to join us."

"We'll follow you."

I reached down and grabbed the one on the end. "You

like to talk so start talking. Where's your friend Gilles?"

He was trying to wiggle away. "Please man . . . don't hurt me. Don't take me to Champagne."

I smirked. "I am Champagne."

"Sh-shittt," he stuttered. I smelled urine. He was pissing himself.

"Where is Lafleur. You tell me, and I'll let you go."

"Keep your trap shut," Torrens said. Then he said in French, "Gilles will kill you."

I smiled and replied in French, "But so will I."

"I'm an idiot, he's French," Torrens said. "Should have spoken in Spanish."

I told him in Spanish that I spoke that language, too. "You guys should do your homework and figure out what languages I speak." I released him.

"Take them in the van," I said to a couple of my guys. "I doubt we'll learn much. These guys are too stupid to live, let alone be a threat. Let the others go."

"You going to kill us?" asked the one who hadn't said a word.

"You killed three friends of mine. What do you think I should do with you?"

"It wasn't me." He shook his head. "I didn't shoot anyone, man." His eyes were filled with fear.

"So, tell me which one?"

Torrens spoke up. "It was all Lafleur. He told us we could get rich off some drugs. He said you stole my sister's land."

"Is that so? Take them out of here." I pushed past the others.

"Where are you going?" Chase asked. Nuts was beside him, waiting.

"I'm going to find Lafleur."

"Not without us, you're not. He's probably long gone," Nuts said. "Why not come with us?"

"Take them back to the clubhouse. I'll be there in a bit." I was on my bike and pulling out of the parking spot before anyone could stop me. Lafleur had been there. I could smell the bastard.

I hunted the streets, up and down. I figured he wouldn't just be hanging around, but I had to be sure. I was angry when I got back to the clubhouse. I walked in the door and Colby came over to me.

"Where the hell did you get to?"

I shook my head. "Don't worry. I'm here now. Where is Torrens?"

"Tied up downstairs."

I pulled up my sleeves. "Okay, it's time to get some answers."

CHAPTER THREE

Colby

I didn't take part in the interrogation of Purnell Torrens, nor did I want to. Those of us not involved lolled around outside. Jerry and I waited, listening to the man's random screams. On the other side of the building stood a few other Banni. As far as I could tell, it would always be us former Death Proof members, and them. Would we ever be a cohesive whole?

As dawn broke, Calvin came out of the building and walked over to us.

"Colby," he said, "I'm worried about yer dad." He had good reason to be, although it seemed weird that another man was being tortured not too far from us, but my father was probably at home sleeping off a bottle of Southern Comfort.

"Any special reason?" I asked. I detected the note of sarcasm in my own voice and appreciated Jerry's quick grin.

Calvin looked pained as he took out a pack of Red Man from his pocket, pulled a few of the dense tobacco leaves and put them in the palm of his hand. He rubbed the pat with two fingers. He had something to say, and I wished he'd spit it out.

My father's a head case. He and Calvin had been just about lifelong motorbike gang club members and clandestine lovers since I was a teen. I have no idea what Calvin sees in him but have long suspected he's as mad as a hatter,

45

too.

"I hear Diego's ma has the Big C," he said, dipping the tobacco between his bottom lip and front teeth.

Aw, geez. I did not want to discuss her with Calvin. Not when he was inviting the Big C into his mouth each time he chewed that shit. He gnawed on the stuff for a bit, spitting a stream of brown juice onto the ground. Man, that was a nasty habit.

"Yeah," I said cautiously because I wasn't sure how much of a secret it was.

"She talked to Cledus some. I had to intervene." Calvin frowned. "As you know, your pa fought me like a rattlesnake on getting cancer treatment for his prostate. He tried to tell her to let nature take its course."

That was shocking news. "Jesus. I can't believe him." I was trying to figure out why Cherise had sought advice from that dingbat Cledus anyway. I constantly shocked me that some people figured because he was still standing that he was some kind of sage. To me, he was the Keith Richards of motorcycle gangs: lucky to be alive. It was an accident, rather than design.

Calvin must have read my apathetic expression, even in the cold morning light. He held up a hand. "He got treatment."

"I know." Where was he going with this? Cledus had made a big deal out of getting Androgen Deprivation Therapy. It was my sister, June Gold, who had encouraged him to seek this remedy, in which he received hormone implants in his prostate area. He'd also been getting radiation when the ADT stopped working. As far as I knew he was in the clear.

Calvin sighed. "Your pa never completed the program. He's still got cancer. Stage four. He's the last one that oughta be givin' advice to Cherise."

Oh, man. I had no idea he was so sick, but I was relieved Calvin agreed with me about Cledus not being a role model for Diego's ailing mother.

A shrill scream stopped all conversation.

"I don't know! I don't know!" a man yelled from the basement. I shuddered.

Calvin shook his head. "He's not hittin' him hard enough if the prick can still talk." He gave me another sigh. "I'm gonna go supervise." He donned leather gloves. I knew what that meant. Torrens would get a severe beating to his kidneys and liver, but the leather wouldn't leave a mark. If he survived his ordeal, Torrens would piss blood for a week and feel like hell, but his torturers would get what they wanted.

"The point is, son—"

I am not your son.

"Make sure she gets to the hospital tomorrow." He flicked a gaze up at the lightening sky. "I should say, today. She's starting all the prep work. Near as I can tell, they got her early. Stage one. That's the good news. She says it's an aggressive form of cancer, but it's still stage one."

He dropped his voice and leaned closer to me. His breath would have killed an ox.

"I understand she's scared, but she needs someone there." He glanced in the direction of where another scream arose. "And it shouldn't be Diego. She doesn't want him to see her vulnerable."

"Okay." I winced as he cracked his knuckles and went off to cause some grievous bodily harm.

Silence permeated the air.

"Think he's still alive?" Jerry asked, sounding nervous.

"I don't know." Man, we'd just buried three guys. We needed to open our own mortuary at this rate.

Jerry and I waited because that's what we were supposed

to do. The other guys eventually ambled over to us.

"Think he's dead?" Marcel asked.

Man, we were a morbid bunch these days.

Ten minutes later, Calvin came out, a weird look on his face. A couple of the Banni guys followed, Diego propped between them. There was blood all over his face and chest.

"S'okay," Diego mumbled to me. "Stu went for Torrens with a knife and aimed too wide and got me instead."

He seemed to be in shock.

"He needs stitches," Calvin said.

"And Torrens?" Jerry asked.

"He needs a body bag." Calvin looked at me. "Get him seen to. I'll take Diego over to the hospital. You take care of that other piece of business, we discussed, okay?"

It took me a moment to recover my composure. He and my dad had been pretty rough guys in their day, but never this bad. Or were they and I just didn't see it?

"Are you cut bad?" I asked Diego. He really didn't look so good.

He shook his head. "I'm fine. Honest."

Calvin made a tsking sound. "I called the hospital, and there's a big, fancy plastic surgeon there. Came in to work on some mucky-muck who got into a car accident. He's waiting for us now."

I couldn't act too upset about Diego's condition, even though I did worry about all the blood on him.

"We got what we needed," Calvin told the group. "Torrens told us where Lafleur is. He's holed up in a state-of-the-art underground bunker at Teresa's tomato farm." He snorted, dangling a set of keys with a telltale BMW emblem on them. "Whoever said crime doesn't pay?"

He walked off with Diego leaning on him and Stu. That left the rest of us to clean up the basement.

"This outta be fun." Jerry rolled his eyes.

We all trooped downstairs. My cell phone rang. It was Calvin. I took the call.

He dropped his voice. "Diego doesn't want his mom to see him like this. Don't tell her he got cut."

I wasn't planning to. I ended the call and took in the scene. It looked like a bloodbath, and the stench of body fluids was overwhelming. We cleaned up as best we could, getting the crumpled body of Purnell Torrens into a roll of industrial plastic.

Two of the guys carted him out of there. Where they took him, I had no idea, and I didn't ask questions. The less I knew, the better, for my mental health, and any possible ramifications. I'd never seen body counts like the ones the Banni racked up. Death Proof had simply never done business this way. I began to miss my old life, except it didn't have Diego in it.

As I threaded a hose through the basement window and gave the place a thorough cleaning with Jerry sweeping up behind me, I decided I didn't want to live this life anymore. I saw no future in the gang wars, the hatred, the lies.

I saw freedom in riding, but for me, the cost had become too high.

Jerry and I rode away, tossing the broom and cleaning supplies into scattered dumpsters. I wanted to wash the dead man's life-blood from my body, and my mind. Jerry went home to his mom's, and I went to Cherise's house, where my dog greeted me like I was Harry Styles, the Beatles, and Justin Timberlake all wrapped up in one skinny package.

It was a little after six in the morning, and the sky was a pale peach. Thinking of peaches made me think of my sister. Not June Gold—named for a special variety of Texas peach—the one living and working in New Orleans. The one who was being an absolute bitch right now.

No. It made me think of my little Garnet Beauty, also named for a Texas peach. She was my cherished and adored sister, who'd vanished without a trace fifteen-and-a-half years ago. She'd been six at the time. My crazy mother had left my dad and taken the girls with her a few years earlier. I'd gone slowly bonkers after too many beatings from Cledus and ran away from home. I missed my sisters badly and went off to see them. They didn't live that far from us, just over an hour's drive in St. John's Parish, but it might have been a million miles.

I was shocked to find that Garnet had gone missing three years before. I called my father, who contacted the police. The detective at the time, Rogan Duchesne, has never given up searching for her. I haven't stopped believing we'll find her but have recently come to accept that she is probably dead.

Partly, it was my sister June's confession that our insane mother, now locked up in a mental facility, had kept Garnet in a cage. She'd abused her and withheld food and love. I still cannot get over that neither of my parents had reported her missing. As long as I live, I will never forgive them or forget their treachery. Cledus claims he didn't know the gruesome details of Garnet's captivity or her disappearance, but how could he not? June Gold told me she'd said something to our father.

Why hadn't he done something before it was too late? Had he not taken June Gold seriously? Then again, knowing what a selfish ass he is, maybe he really didn't keep tabs on her even though June told him what was going on at our mother's house.

Either way, Cledus and Evangeline were stinking, lousy parents who should never have had children. Last time I'd seen my mother was a few days ago, at Duchesne's insistence. He'd sought my permission to authorize the exhumation of two Jane Doe bodies that matched my sister's description. One was in Alabama, the other in Georgia.

I'd gladly signed all the permission forms since I'd always been his go-to guy in my family. He'd put things into motion and asked me to press June Gold for more details of Garnet's last days in Evangeline's house. That's when she told me about the cage.

Meanwhile, the body in Georgia turned out not to be a match. It hadn't even been a child's body but that of a small, pregnant woman with a cleft palate. Authorities had turned their efforts toward Alabama, and I'd gone to see Evangeline, whose mental illness has progressed so rapidly she has gone from assisted living to full lockdown.

Her infatuated case doctor tried to tell me she'd kept Garnet caged to protect her from her. He said Evangeline has suffered from untreated postpartum depression all these years. Seeing her again had been a jolt. Watching as she spanked a doll on her lap and the viciousness in her eyes when she said it was 'Colby' had sent me running from the room.

I'd known it would be futile trying to talk to her, but I would do anything for my sister. I could still see her clearly in my mind. I remembered our last day together before my world turned black. We'd been in the kitchen, and it was a warm, sunny day and Tal Bachman's song, 'She's So High' was on the radio. I'd loved that song. I sang it to Garnet, who laughed, dancing a little jig with me. She'd been wearing only her underpants, her belly slightly protruding, the way little girls' bellies do. She'd wiggled her tush as I sang and beat pancake batter with a spoon.

I guess that song proved to be true. Garnet Beauty was and always will be high above me. I miss her desperately. I both hope she's the kid in Alabama, and dread it, too. I want her to be alive. I want to hug her and love her. I want to grow old with her, reminding each other of the good times, and bad. But I will also settle for closure because that's what desperate people do.

In the meantime, I would wait. And wait.

My dog, Beauty, gave me kisses as I fed her and gave her the last of the bully sticks that I'd bought her. Severe abuse from her former human and I use that word loosely, had knocked out some of her teeth, but she could still chew, and a bully stick occupied her for hours.

She licked the tip of my nose and ran off with her treasure, tucking herself into a corner of Cherise's sofa.

I showered and changed and came out to find her gnawing on the stick. She knew just by my expression that it was Beauty time. She jumped from her perch, and I took her for a quick run, that stick clenched between her smiling teeth.

Lord, I love that dog. Only for her would I slow down and walk. She had to stop and sniff every flower and leaf on the side of the road. She gently licked morning dew from blades of grass and buried her nose in the soft center of countless black-eyed-Susans. A jackrabbit crossed our path, and my big, bad pit bull shook like jelly and dashed behind me, peering at the tiny, scurrying critter from around my leg.

I coaxed her beside me. No good trying to convince her the rabbit was more afraid of her than she was of it. I made encouraging sounds and slowly walked back home, wondering how anyone could have hurt such a precious girl. We made it through the backdoor just as Cherise came down to the kitchen.

"Coffee would be so great." She pulled a face. "But I can't have any on account of my tests."

"I'll buy you breakfast right after it. I'm taking you to the hospital," I told her.

"Where's Diego?"

"Finishing some club business. He asked me to take you."

"Is he hurt?" Her gaze on me was intense.

Man, what could I say? Was she psychic, or what?

"He's okay. I promise." Am I lying to her? I thought about the blood and shook it from my thoughts. We closed up the house, leaving Beauty in the kitchen with her bully stick. Cherise's nervousness ramped up my own as she handed me the keys to her old Buick. We got inside, and I couldn't believe it. The song on the radio was 'She's So High.'

I knew then, more than anything, I wanted Cherise to be okay, both for Diego and for me.

Her cell phone rang, and I could have predicted it would be Diego. She relaxed completely hearing her son's voice. After a brief conversation, he asked to speak to me, and as I approached the parking lot of the Mary Bird Perkins Cancer Treatment Center, I took the phone from her.

"Hey," he said.

The silence that fell between us had me thinking about how badly I wanted to kiss him and hold him.

"Huh," he said, as though reading my thoughts.

Another pause. I walked with Cherise, who began to look pale. I knew she was frightened, and I would have been, too.

"So, I had a fantastic surgeon," Diego said. "I got four stitches, and he promised me I wouldn't have a scar." A pause. "Calvin's a freak, Colby."

"Yeah, I know."

"He beat that guy to death, and Torrens fought every inch of the way. Sometimes I get so sick of this crap."

I didn't say, *me too*, though it was on the tip of my tongue.

"I'll be at the hospital when I can." He sighed. "I gotta go find Lafleur before he comes after me." And with that, he ended our call.

We walked inside, and Cherise said, "I don't want him

coming here. I want him to think of me as proud and strong."

"You are proud and strong." I took her hand as we approached the Oncology unit. The nursing staff was friendly, and the hospital felt so much more cheerful than the place my mother now calls home.

A nurse put us in a small conference room and weighed Cherise. "You've dropped two pounds since last week." She threw Cherise an accusatory look. "Are you eating?"

Cherise looked absolutely petrified as she sat close to me. I squeezed her hand to reassure her. "I can't eat." She lapsed into a nervous silence. "But I have quit smoking, just like the doctor said I should."

I had never seen her smoking and wondered when she managed to do it.

As if on cue, the door opened, and a very handsome young doctor walked in. As the nurse took Cherise's blood pressure and drew several vials of blood, the doctor sat across the table from us and introduced himself as Dr. Pressman.

"You're very lucky we caught this so early," he said. "As you know, it's stage one, and I believe with immediate, multi-dimensional treatment, we can beat this thing."

We. As far as I knew, the cancer was hers, not his. He sort of irritated me but I said nothing. Cherise squeezed my hand this time, as though agreeing with me. Could she read my thoughts?

"Your doctor referred you to me because this is my specialty, Mrs. Champagne."

"Please, call me Cherise."

"All right then. Cherise." He opened an iPad and spun it around so that she could see different images on the screen.

"There are several different types of treatment we can use since we've caught this so early, but I'd like to start immediately with hormone therapy. We can give you this in pill form."

He went on about something called aromatase inhibitors. "We plan to attack the tumor, which is isolated to one spot, with hormones to slow its growth."

The doctor flicked through several shots of x-rays. "We'll put you on a high dosage for a week, then check your blood levels and do an MRI.

"We'll take an ultrasound exactly one week from today to see if the tumor has shrunk at all. Then we can discuss our next options. My hope is to avoid surgery, but if not, the good news is that we should be able to do laparoscopic surgery, which will reduce your recovery time. We would then follow up with immediate radiation treatment."

"Will I need chemotherapy?"

"I hope not. By using these different modalities, we should be able to avoid it, especially since we're nipping it in the bud, so to speak." He smiled at her. "Any questions?"

Cherise had plenty. She wanted to know about the side effects of the hormone treatment.

"Well, you will find an increased appetite."

"Oh, great," she muttered.

"Weight gain—"

"Super."

"And fluid retention."

"Awesome!"

The doctor and I looked at each other, then at her. Finally, she smiled. We all laughed, which broke up the tension between us.

"I'll see you in a week," he said, after answering a few more questions.

When he left us alone, she sat back in her chair and let out a breath. "I could just do nothing and let nature take its course."

"You will not," I said. "Diego needs you." I was still holding her hand, and I lifted it to my lips and kissed it. "I need you."

She gazed at me. "Maybe the hormones will work. Maybe that's all I need."

"Yeah, maybe. But whatever you need, I'll be with you here all the way."

The doctor returned with two prescriptions. "This one is for progesterone. The second one is for hydrochlorothiazide, to help with the fluid retention." He flicked a glance at me.

"Make sure she takes them. She's beautiful but feisty, this one." He gave her a wink, and she turned all moon-faced. He gave her a beautiful smile and left again.

"Dang," she said. "I think he just woke up my girly bits."

I laughed. "And a good thing, too. How about I buy you some coffee and pancakes, and we'll wash down your pills?"

She pulled a face. "I'm supposed to be on greens. I have nightmares about broccoli. I'd love some coffee and um . . ." She curled a stray strand of hair behind her ear. "I've been reading about this place called Another Broken Egg. Their breakfast is supposed to be amazing. They have a sweet potato pancake that they serve with cinnamon-infused syrup. Doesn't that sound healthy?"

No. "Sounds great to me. Where is it?"

"It's on Citicourt Drive." She seemed happier than I'd seen her in days as we went to the pharmacy, picked up her medicines, then drove out to the corporate section of Baton Rouge. Another Broken Egg might have been intended for tourists, nestled as it was between a Best Western, a Richmond Inn, and a deli, but the menu was pure southern decadence.

She ordered her longed-for coffee and sweet potato pancakes, and I went for the shrimp and grits.

"I really miss smoking," Cherise told me as the waitress

took off with our orders.

"When did you quit?"

"Last night." She gave me a wicked grin.

I burst out laughing. Her cell phone rang, and I was pleased to see the mischief sparkling in her eyes as she talked to Diego.

He didn't ask to speak to me this time, and it was probably just as well. I missed him. Too damned much.

Cherise ended their call. My cell phone rang just as our coffees arrived. Duchesne. I knew before I even spoke to him that he had the news I'd both dreaded and always hoped for.

"There's no easy way to tell you this, Colby, but we have a match. We found your baby girl."

I sat with the news a moment, unable to respond.

"I'm at the University of Alabama in Tuscaloosa. It's about an hour away from Birmingham."

When I didn't respond, he continued. "I'm with the forensic pathology unit which services the City of Birmingham and the surrounding region. This is one of the finest units in the country servicing the Jefferson County Coroner and Medical Examiner's Office." He took a breath, and his voice wobbled. "Would you like to come out here?"

"Yes."

"I know you love your chopper but I'm almost four hundred miles from you, and it would take you about five and a half, maybe six hours by road. See if you can grab a flight to Birmingham and I'll pick you up and drive you here. You going to come alone?"

"Is everything okay?" Cherise asked, reaching out to me. Her gaze looked stricken. I realized I was crying. She stroked my arm. "It's okay, it's okay, sweetheart."

But it was not. The last shred of belief in life being a beautiful thing had just been ripped away from me.

"You still there?" Duchesne asked.

"Yeah."

"You going to come alone?" he asked again.

"No." There was only one person I would want to accompany me, and that was Diego, but I couldn't ask him. The only other person in the world I would ever want in a moment like this was—

"Jerry," I said.

Duchesne repeated his name. "Don't talk to anyone else. Nobody else in your family. We need this contained."

That worried me. "Is it... is Garnet Beauty really the body in the cooler?"

"Yes." He sounded terse. "Get the first flight you can and let me know your arrival time. I'll be waiting for you." He ended the call.

I was a mess. My eyes swam, then tears began to fall down my cheeks and into my food. My hands shook. I called Jerry, who manned up and started calling around for flights. Cherise kept talking to me, hugging me. I think she kind of kept all the broken pieces in me pulled together in her loving ministrations. I couldn't get over how lost and desolate I felt. I'd waited for, and wanted news, but not this. Not really. I wanted her to be alive.

Cherise called Diego, who didn't pick up. She left him a message, and I paid the check for the meal that still hadn't arrived by the time we left.

"I'm so sorry," I told Cherise, who was amazing. She drove me to Sue-Ellen's house. As we pulled up, I realized that in spite of the warmth of the day Cherise had ramped up the heat in the car. I was still shaking, and I knew it was from shock.

Sue-Ellen came out, a look of anguish on her face. She opened the door, pulled me out, and held me, saying comforting things.

"Nobody can touch her anymore, Colby. She's in God's arms now, flying with the angels."

High above me. Yes, she was.

Sue-Ellen pushed herself away from me and cupped my face in her hands. "You go bring our little girl home, and if your father asks, I'll tell him you and Jerry have gone fishing or something."

Those two fantastic women drove me and Jerry to the airport. We made our Delta flight just in time, and for the three and a half hours we were in the air since there were no direct flights, my mind was in turmoil. Tears kept leaking from my eyes. God bless Jerry. He held my hand each time I became unglued but said nothing. There was nothing to say. No words could ease the hurt.

He was just there. Just Jerry. Like he'd always been.

Duchesne didn't have much to say either when he picked us up at Birmingham-Shuttlesworth Airport and drove us to the university. He focused on the road, driving quickly.

"How you doin'?" he asked when we stopped at a red light.

"Okay." I took a deep breath. "Have you seen her?"

A slow nod. His eyes turned bright, but he didn't say anything. I wondered if he was thinking about his own sister, Lark, who'd gone missing as she hitchhiked out in the Nevada desert years earlier. Each of us having a missing sister had drawn us close to one another from the beginning. And now, one of us would be getting ready for a funeral.

Jerry sat in back, occasionally reaching over to squeeze my shoulder. The longer the drive went on, the more I started to realize how far we were from Baton Rouge. Whoever had transported Garnet Beauty here had driven a long, long way from home.

"I'm going to show you the dump site," Duchesne suddenly said, then paused. "Shit. That sounded terrible."

"But true," I responded.

"I haven't told you much because we weren't sure until today that the little girl the local authorities dubbed Baby Jane Doe was your sister. The cops worked hard to solve the mystery but had no luck. They cared so much they even paid for a grave for her. I'll show you that, too, then I'll let the medical examiner explain the forensics."

"Okay." My mind sorted through all the people I knew who could have brought her out here. As we swung off the highway, turned off at a truck stop and then plunged down to a verdant trail boasting a sign that read Welcome to Moss Rock Preserve, I knew. I knew who had left my baby sister alone in a goddamned water cooler.

My precious Garnet Beauty who'd been afraid of the dark. Alone, out here.

"Damn," I said. Fresh tears pricked my eyes.

"I know it sucks, man." Duchesne put his hand on my shoulder, but I got out of the car and stood, alert, waiting for his direction. He pointed to a cluster of trees.

"They found the water cooler in there. Two hikers found it. It was lying on its side. It was a hot morning, and they saw water and what looked like Coca-Cola pooled around it. They noticed the stench as they got closer." Duchesne let out a sigh.

"The detectives investigating the incident theorized that whoever killed the little girl, placed her body in the cooler and covered her with Coke cans and ice to mask their crime.

"The summer sun not only melted the ice but also popped the soda cans, which destroyed a lot of forensic evidence. An autopsy later disclosed she had been smothered and had been dead about a week. There were signs of sexual abuse and . . ." He paused. "Starvation and torture."

"Calvin," I said. "Calvin was a truck driver back then." I shook my head. "He's the only one I know who could have a plausible reason for being gone a few days. My father disappeared all the time, but never for that long. But I'm having a hard time believing he had anything to do with this." I looked at him. "Am I wrong?"

"No. No, Colby. You are not."

CHAPTER FOUR

Her grave almost broke me in pieces. I stared at it for several minutes. It had been opened, desecrated, but the black headstone, which leaned against a tree, left me devastated. They had, as Duchesne had told me, called her Baby Jane Doe. Underneath the name, the words Because We Care were etched into the stone.

"There were two detectives who worked this case," Duchesne told me. "They are still haunted by it. They've been waiting for a resolution."

"I'd like to meet them," I said. I found it hard to keep upright. I wanted to hurl myself onto the ground. I wanted to be with her.

It wasn't fair. It was just so wrong. Why did God keep serial killers and child molesters alive and yet allowed innocent babies to die?

"I can arrange that." Duchesne's voice was quiet. "You're doing great, my friend. I know this is not how we wanted to find her."

No, it wasn't. I wanted summer kisses, not autumn leaves falling to the ground. I kept thinking of the song 'Autumn Leaves.' I missed her so much. The days had been so long without her.

How could I live without her?

What had kept me going was the faint hope that she was alive. I couldn't quite accept the truth yet. I would in time, but numbness had set in. I suppose it's what happens. Nature's way of helping us cope with the impossible.

My darling girl was gone.

Duchesne and Jerry were great. We hugged each other. All three of us cried.

"When all this is over can I take her home and bury her?" I asked. I didn't want her to be alone anymore.

"Yes, of course. It might take a couple of weeks." Duchesne flicked me a glance. "Are you sure you're up to going to the forensic pathologist's office?"

I nodded. I had to be. But now I felt really sick. Back in the car, I felt like crap. I wanted to barf and asked Duchesne to pull over on the highway. I threw up, but I hadn't eaten and had barely consumed a cup of coffee that morning. Still, I felt much better for it.

Turning my thoughts toward Calvin, I wondered if my dad knew of his lover's part in this. Had he killed her? Or had he showed up to merely eliminate the evidence?

We drove to the university, and the dreadful chill that had swept over me on and off all day consumed me once more.

Jerry and I followed Duchesne through the hushed corridors of the forensic pathology unit.

At a door marked with the number 213, black lettering read Pediatric Forensic Pathology.

Duchesne knocked and, after a faint buzzing sounded, he pushed open the door. I wasn't sure what I'd expected, but nothing could have prepared me for the extensive collection of child skeletons and baby skulls that lined numerous shelves along the walls.

These were obviously real. Some showed deformities. Huge photos and artist sketches filled the spaces above them. With a wrench, I recognized one of the drawings as that of my sister.

One large photo stopped me in my tracks. A young girl's torso was covered in deep wounds, the obvious violence of the attack just astonishing.

"Her father did that." A woman who sat at a bench examining something under a microscope told us. "He said the voices in his head told him it was the only way to drive the devil out of her body."

I swallowed. Hard. Everywhere I looked, I saw utter devastation. How did these people do this job every day? I thanked God they did because people like me needed answers. We needed their help.

"This is Dr. Jane Lacey, and she's the one who has been working on your case," Duchesne said.

"Thank you for helping my friend," Jerry said, shaking her hand when my body refused to cooperate. "You have no idea. This has eaten Colby alive for fifteen years."

"I understand." The empathy, the infinite sadness in her eyes, swept over me. It was real. No more hope. No more wondering. I finally had to accept it was real.

The autumn leaves had fallen, and winter was beginning to set.

"You want coffee?" Duchesne asked me.

I nodded. I needed something warm, even if I wasn't sure I'd be able to keep it down. I sat on a stool beside Jerry as Dr. Lacey explained about Garnet Beauty.

"We tried everything to get identification on her. We wanted to know exactly what your sister went through. To that end, we worked with an anthropologist from the Smithsonian Institute." She gestured to a folder beside her. The artist's rendition of my sister was the same picture high up on the wall. It was the same as the one Duchesne had showed me when he first asked for my signature to authorize the exhumations.

"Does she look like your sister?" Dr. Lacey suddenly asked. "I mean, to you. I've seen photos of her, and I thought it was a pretty good likeness."

"No, not really," I admitted.

Jerry said nothing. He squeezed my shoulder.

Damn. I didn't want to see my Garnet Beauty this way.

"She was skeletal when we found her. Decomposition had been swift," Dr. Lacey said. I detected the defensive tone in her voice. She put her hand on my arm. "You hadn't seen her for a while I am told."

That was true. I nodded.

She pointed to the picture. "It doesn't look like Garnet because probably when you last saw her, she was a healthy, happy little girl."

"Yes. Yes." I kept nodding automatically. I couldn't forget our last morning together, baking in the kitchen.

"The little girl we found . . . well, there's an awful lot of misery and suffering in the face of a child who only lived six years."

The impact of what she said and the realization of my sister's traumatic final months hit me. When I looked at the drawing once more, I saw the pain and anguish. I cursed my stupid parents for not being able to hack marriage. I cursed my mother for taking the girls away from us, but most of all I cursed my father. I felt certain he was somehow responsible for this.

Had he talked Calvin into disposing of Garnet's remains?

"Thank you for everything you've done," I said. Grief gnawed at me. I felt as though it was the last thing I owned.

Nobody said anything for a moment as Duchesne returned with two coffees for me and Jerry.

"Has Detective Duchesne explained about the fingerprints?" Dr. Lacey flicked him a glance that spoke volumes. She had a crush on him, and he was oblivious.

"I think he said that the exploding pop cans inside the cooler destroyed evidence such as DNA and fingerprints." I struggled to remember everything he'd said.

She gave me a small, tight smile. "That is almost true. In any criminal investigation, we leave out some details when we release information to the media. We found a single thumbprint on the outside of the cooler that we were never able to identify. We ran it through AFIS—the Integrated Automated Fingerprint Identification System—several times over the years and never got a hit."

Dr. Lacey looked me in the eye. "Until yesterday." She got up from her table and walked to the other end of the room. I became aware of the frankly curious gazes of other workers in the room. They glanced at me over the tops of microscopes and bones they'd been examining.

A soft click caught my attention. Dr. Lacey returned with the cooler held between her gloved hands. It was pale yellow, with a white lid. It looked too small to have been big enough to hold my sister, but then I had to remind myself she'd been starved and abused.

I wanted to hurt everyone who had participated in her demise. Tears pooled in my eyes as I watched as the pathologist gently laid the cooler on a piece of plastic. She pointed a gloved finger at the underside of the handle on the left side.

"We kept the information about the fingerprint private."

"Was it Calvin's?"

She shook her head. "Let me explain."

I wanted to know who was responsible and I wanted to know now. Then I would fly home, get a gun and kill the motherfucker who did this. It was hard to act calm. But I had to do it.

It was the performance of a lifetime.

A few seconds later, two middle-aged men walked into the room, and Duchesne introduced us. Detective John Stevens retired, and Detective Dan Poole, were the men who had worked so long and hard to solve my sister's murder.

They were the ones who confirmed she'd been raped and strangled and had been apparently severely abused and starved for months.

Detective Poole picked up the story.

"We held a small funeral for Baby Jane Doe, and we told everybody that the funeral did not mean that we were giving up on this case. Far from it. We hoped that over time, whoever did this would come to the grave and visit her. We've had people keeping an eye open on and off. We've had people visit the grave periodically, including on the anniversary of her death. People come to pay their respects.

"We kept hoping it would be the conscience-stricken killer or someone who knew the killer, but no such luck. Every year there was someone who would place a toy, a doll, something to show they remember, but none provided clues."

He let out a sigh. "We thought someday the killer might die and perhaps someone who knows the truth would call us."

I waited because I knew there was some big Aha! moment coming.

"We got a tip-off a couple of weeks ago about the exhumation of Baby Jane Doe's body, and we had a feeling the killer would find out. We put hidden cameras in strategic places around the grave. With Detective Duchesne's permission, we waited twenty-four hours before digging her up."

"And?" Jerry prompted, practically falling off his chair.

"He came."

"Who?" I asked.

"Calvin," Duchesne interjected.

"So, it's his thumbprint?" I asked. "Because Dr. Lacey said it wasn't."

"Before I tell you whose fingerprint it was, I want you to know that until Detective Duchesne supplied us with your family's fingerprints, we had no idea whose thumb it was on the cooler."

I began to think fast. It couldn't have been my dad's because he was certainly in the criminal justice system. They would have tapped him years ago. It wasn't me. That left my mom and my sister.

"Shit. June Gold," I said.

Dr. Lacey nodded. "There was something else we left out of the media release. We found a store receipt. At the time we felt it had fluttered to the bottom of the ravine where it was found, unseen, by whoever left it there. The body, sorry, your sister, was dumped in the dark, and the killer didn't see it. It's a miracle we found the receipt but what's spooky is we found another one right after Calvin left."

She pulled a glassine envelope out of her folder, and I studied the two receipts.

Spooky didn't even begin to cut it.

The receipts were similar except the old one was missing pertinent information such as the name of the store. It wasn't time-stamped either. Somebody had purchased a brand-new drink cooler, a dozen cans of coke, two ice packs, and a six-pack of Coors Light.

Calvin's receipt showed a purchase of a six-pack of Coors Light. I tried to think back to the date he'd purchased the beer. It was the night Diego, and I found Beauty at the mobile dog rescue.

God, how chilling was that? I'd adopted Beauty, thinking that it was sad and ironic that she had my sister's name.

I sat studying the receipts. It looked like they came from a truck stop on the border between Louisiana and Alabama.

"We found the first receipt two weeks after we found the body. Somebody turned it in," Dr. Lacey said.

"Who found it?" I asked.

"A hiker. But the night before we exhumed the body,

Calvin went to the grave. He sat there for a long time, drinking beer. He mowed through a six-pack, probably knowing the outcome of the inquiry. Probably wondering what to do next."

Duchesne pushed some surprisingly clear surveillance photos toward me on the worktable. Calvin seemed comfortable enough sitting at the foot of the grave chugging beers. He looked like he was talking to somebody.

Who?

And then I saw her, June Gold. She appeared to be yelling at him. He picked up his cans and left, but they forgot the receipt. There was a final photo of the receipt right near Garnet Beauty's grave.

"Wow," I said. "I don't even know what to say."

"Fifteen years ago, we didn't have a way to test for a child's fingerprints once they'd been left longer than three weeks. It's a little-known fact of law enforcement. Techniques have developed since then. We were able to lift two more prints from Garnet Beauty's body. One was on her yellow hairclip still in her hair. And one was from — "

She stopped speaking.

"Where?" I asked, hearing my own voice cracking.

"Masking tape. Somebody put it across her eyes."

"Dear God." Jerry looked stricken.

I wanted to kill Calvin and my sister.

I also knew I was going to throw up again and I'd only had two sips of coffee. I excused myself and went to the john. I felt better after the second barfing, but I think it had more to do with the fact that I received a call from Diego.

"What's going on?" he asked.

I told him.

"You coming home soon?" he responded.

"Not sure."

"Stay in touch with me. Lafleur is on the run. He's apparently lookin' to kill you. And me. Somehow he figured out you're important to me."

"Am I?"

"Shaddap," he said.

I actually grinned.

"Stay safe." He sounded worried. Not his usual suave self. "I've relocated Cherise and Beauty to a safe house. I'll feel better when you're there, too." He paused. "And babe? I'd love to be the one that takes out that sick fuck Calvin."

"Don't forget my sister. She's a piece of work, too."

"I'll have somebody watch her over there in N'Orleans. I'm gonna keep an eye on Calvin myself."

"I wish you'd keep an eye on me," I grumped.

"Huh," he said and hung up.

Duchesne and the other detectives urged secrecy and silence on the results of the lab tests. Big oops. I'd already told Diego, but I knew we could trust him. I was the one who couldn't be trusted.

If I flew back home, Calvin would be dead, and my sister would be in deep shit.

Duchesne insisted that Jerry and I stay the night and secured us rooms in a motel by the Birmingham airport. Fine by me. He had a room, too. The place wasn't exactly the Bates Motel, but it wasn't the Ritz-Carlton, either.

"Don't leave town," Duchesne said. "Please let the authorities do their thing. We'll have Calvin and June arrested. I'm having your old man pulled, too. I can't believe he knew nothing about this."

I was pretty sure he knew everything. The slimy grease bag that he was.

Crashing on my bed, I tried watching the news on TV. I almost laughed over a report of a bicyclist getting hit by a bus on the highway in Tuscaloosa. He'd been bent over looking for his false teeth at the time.

I fell asleep, my dreams pained and exhausting.

Awakened sometime later by a pounding at the door, I wondered fleetingly if it might be Lafleur. I would have really given him what-for. I checked the grimy peephole.

Man, what a sight for sore eyes.

Diego stood on the other side, giving me a finger wave. After snatching open the door, I grabbed him.

"Get in here," I said.

He let me pull him into my arms, and I slammed the door closed. The lamps and grim artwork on the walls would have jumped, but everything had been nailed down. Clearly, this motel dealt with a really classy type of clientele.

Our mouths landed on each other's. We traded lingering, wet kisses. Without a word being exchanged, I stripped my man and stared at his naked body.

"Come to Papa," I crooned, wrapping my fist around his length.

He glanced down at his erect cock, so hard it was pointing up toward his belly.

"I drove like hell to get here. I had to see you. I thought we could talk," he muttered, shaking his head at his cock. "Guess that's gonna have to wait."

"No, no. We can talk. Let me start."

He seemed suddenly bashful as I pushed him to the small table for two with its mismatched chairs that overlooked the glamorous parking lot.

Diego started to say something as I bent him over the tabletop, but I had words I wanted to say myself. And I drew them in tongue against his hot ass cheeks. I loved the taste and smell of him. A little bit spicy. A little bit musky. A whole lot of Southern comfort. And I don't mean the boozy kind. More the woozy kind. He was soft, hard, and everything in between.

He jerked at my touch but manfully stayed where he was.

I took my time sucking his bubble butt, finally delving into the crack. He let out a moan that touched my very soul. It made me think of the Prince song, 'When Doves Cry.' I teased him with kisses, licks, then spread his cheeks with my fingers, focusing on his glorious hole. I shoved one of his knees upward so that he looked like he was climbing the table.

Sensing his gaze on me, I lifted my face away from him and glanced up at him. He had twisted his head around and looked down at me, a feverish expression on his face. I lost no time pleasuring him again. I stabbed my tongue at his hole. He kept rubbing it against me, anxious for closer contact. I slipped a finger into him, then a second, alternating with my tongue. I was able to stick it into him, making him moan once again. But then I pushed his ass all the way up onto the table, almost tipping it over.

"Oh, God, suck me," he rasped, as we straightened the table together. He held on for dear life, legs open as I swooped down on him again. This time I swabbed his rigid cock, making him squirm. His chest heaved with the effort to breathe. Good. By the time I was done with him, he'd be rode hard and put away wet, as the saying goes. I paid a bit of attention to his huge balls, lurking near the edge of the table, and resumed fucking him with two fingers. With them embedded in his ass, I was able to focus on his cock, and he went bonkers when I finally slipped my mouth over his rigid length. He grabbed my head, almost sending the table to the floor again, but we held on, rocking and reeling as I sucked him harder, faster.

And then he came. He roared as he exploded in my throat, his legs flailing around my head. He grabbed my ears, as though I might stop sucking him.

Not a chance.

I waited until his spasms subsided and then I released his

cock with great reluctance.

"You're trying to kill me," he said between ragged pants.

I didn't respond. I pushed his legs back up toward his chest. His feet landed on my shoulders. We locked gazes between his open legs, and I began to fuck him with my fingers again.

He whispered, "Fuck," as my tongue delved in around my fingers. "Oh, Colby."

I kept a steady pace as he writhed around on the table, working up a serious sweat. When I claimed his cock a second time, he went nuts, until I let him go. I worked my way back to his balls and ass, and he humped my face and fingers. I sucked his cock back into my mouth again several minutes later, and he rewarded me with more of his sweet juices.

"You know, we should finish this in bed." I moved away from his butt, pulled him into my arms and onto the bed, which had definitely seen better days.

"I think I feel a spring in my back," he said, laughing as I took his face in my hands and kissed him. Another spring shot up right near his shoulder. We both laughed, but really, talk about a passion killer.

"Oh, man. What a crummy dump this is. I'm so sorry, Diego."

"Oh, for fuck's sake, shut up, get naked and put your cock inside me."

"I'll get naked, but I am nowhere near ready to fuck you." He'd never asked me to do it before, and I almost went mad with need.

My cell phone rang, and I would have ignored it, except that somebody was knocking at the same time.

"Open up. It's me," Duchesne yelled, hammering louder now. Diego flew off the bed, throwing on clothes. Sirens wailed outside. What the hell was going on?

When Diego was dressed, I opened the door.

"You're both here. Good." Duchesne cut a glance from me to Diego and back again.

"What happened?" I asked.

"Somebody's gone on a homicidal rampage back in Baton Rouge. Somebody blew Calvin away, and your sister's bakery in New Orleans got shot to shit. She and her husband have disappeared."

I thought my heart would stop beating. "What about the kids?" I asked. The pain in my chest was so bad I thought I was having a heart attack. I clutched the doorframe.

"They're okay. Henry and Garnet Beauty were found. Tied to their beds but they're alive. We explained to Children and Family Services that you are the next of kin and they will take them into protective custody until we can get you to them."

"Holy shit," I said. "What kind of asshole ties two little kids to their beds?"

The same kind of asshole that helps to kill a little girl and tosses her away in a water cooler.

"Breathe," Diego said, his arm going under mine.

It was the last thing I remembered as I fell down in a dead faint.

CHAPTER FIVE

Diego

We drove back to Baton Rouge in the van. They say when it rains, it pours. It wasn't just pouring right now, there was a goddamned flood, and I felt like I was drowning in it. My mother was really sick, and Lafleur was on the hunt for me, and anyone else he imagined might cause me pain if he killed them. Then there was Colby's family, who, it had turned out, was involved with the murder of his youngest sister.

After all that hot sex earlier, Colby and I had had one hell of a fight. Colby naturally wanted to go right away and pick up his niece and nephew from Child and Family Services. It took some doing on my part to make him see what a terrible idea that was. I knew if Colby took the kids now, they'd be in danger, too. As far as I could tell, Lafleur knew nothing about them, and I wanted to keep it that way. I'd had guys keeping an eye on June Gold and her family in New Orleans, but the reports kept coming back that there was no sign of trouble.

Not from Lafleur anyway. Once the police went after June Gold, there would be. But first things first.

Colby finally saw it my way and agreed to let me take him to the safe house to be with Cherise, but he wasn't happy when he got into the van I'd driven from Baton Rouge to Birmingham.

"I hate this thing. At least you didn't hogtie me this time," he groused as we made good time on the freeway.

My emotions were in shreds. I was worried about my mother. She was being treated for cancer and hiding from a psycho at the same time. Talk about stress. I had a guy out for my blood and everyone around me, and possibly a traitor in my midst. Now Colby was pissed at me.

I had to put all these emotions stirring round inside me into a little box somewhere and lock them away. I had to be the leader of the Banni. If I didn't stop feeling like a hurt little boy, I'd be lost, and Lafleur would have the upper hand. I needed to think. And believe me, there were many questions swirling around my mind, like how Lafleur knew that Colby meant anything more to me than any of the other members.

That question was eating at me. I tried to think of who could have known that Colby and I were secret lovers, and who wanted me dead. Of course Chase came to mind. There was Cledus, too, who wouldn't cry at my funeral, but I doubted that either of them knew my and Colby's secret.

I began to get angry, and suspicious, and those feelings thankfully gutted all the others that made me sad and scared. But getting rid of the feeling I didn't want to have wasn't tough for me. I was used to denying any feelings that made me vulnerable, like fear and anxiety. As a boy, I'd learned to swallow my trepidation when someone from the bank came round threatening to take the house. After they'd leave, I'd comfort my hysterical mother and tell her that I'd make sure no one would ever take our house. I learned how to stop myself from throwing up when I watched some guy cut another man's throat in the middle of a screaming crowd. Then after it was over, I'd clean up the blood. And I was only twelve years old.

As Colby sat beside me now in the club's van, I was well on my way to putting up the barriers again. I couldn't think about Colby's pain or his little sister and what'd been done to her. If I did, I wouldn't have let the police go after them. I'd have done it myself. And vengeance wouldn't bring that little girl back or take away Colby's pain.

Colby's agony was the worst. I could take my own, but to watch others I loved suffer, that was hardest not to feel. When Colby had pulled me into that the motel room two hours or so ago, I knew he needed me. I was a distraction, a way for him to deal with the anguish. I was prepared to give him whatever he wanted in that room, but there was nothing that could erase what had happened. If I'd thought stringing up Calvin, Colby's old man and his sister would bring back that little girl, I wouldn't have hesitated.

I reached over and placed my hand over his. I expected him to pull away. He didn't. Instead, Colby turned his head and looked at me.

I was surprised when he linked his fingers with mine. I could feel his gaze on me as I drove. He was silently asking me something. I don't know why I could hear him, but I could. "I can't," I said softly, my eyes on the road.

"What?" Colby replied. "I didn't say anything."

"You didn't have to."

"So, it's come to that, has it? You read my mind now." He released my hand.

I didn't answer.

"Aside from your cock, what is it you think I want from you, Diego?"

"Right now, it seems you want to fight with me."

"No."

"Yeah, you do. And I understand why. Anger is better than sadness."

"You're Dr. Freud now."

"No, but I've had a little bit of experience with pain. Anyway, let's not go there."

"Go where?" he demanded.

"Drop it. I have a lot on my mind right now."

"Yeah, I know."

I glanced at him again. I heard something in his voice bordering on sarcasm.

He looked at me. "A lot of things, like torturing people and getting stitches and . . . that sort of thing, which wasn't what I signed up for."

"What is it exactly you signed up for, Colby? You knew what you were getting into. I never sugarcoated it. The Banni offered Death Proof protection. Did you think we spent our time sending flowers and candy and writing romantic sonnets?" Now it was my turn to be sarcastic.

"I don't want this anymore." His hands were balled up into fists.

"Well, it's too late for that. The minute you decided to catcall to me that day I was headed to the bike rally in Texas, you set the course."

"Sometimes I wish I'd never laid eyes on you."

I swallowed the hurt and reacted in my usual way, pissed off. "There's the Colby I know and love. Hot and cold, like after the first time you invited me to your room, fucked the hell out of me, and left me on the bedroom floor."

He didn't comment.

I stopped at a red light and checked my rearview. "Shit," I said softly between my teeth.

"What is it?" Colby stiffened.

"I saw that vehicle a while back. Could be nothing." I reached under the seat for my gun and put it between my legs. "Undo your seatbelt and get down."

"Are you serious?"

The car beside me turned left, leaving the space open beside me.

"Do it!" As Colby quickly released his belt, I shoved his head down with one hand. I picked up the gun with the other. The black Trans Am moved up beside me on the driver's side.

A blast of gunfire flew through the window. I ducked, managing to get a view of the car from the side mirror. I lifted the gun and fired back several shots, then I turned the wheel, went through the red and headed down a side street in the wrong lane. A barrage of horns honked. I heard the squeal of brakes, and I lifted my head as high as I dared and put my foot to floor.

"Colby? Are you all right?"

"Yeah," he managed, wiping the shards of glass off his hair.

"Stay down."

I got out of the wrong lane as fast as I could and kept going. I checked behind me. The vehicle had gone. Either I'd hit him, or he'd decided not to pursue me.

My breathing began to return to normal. "Fuck."

"What was that?" Colby glanced up at me.

"You can get up now."

I checked the mirrors in every direction. Eventually, I slowed down. All I needed was a ticket. I made a detour through an alley and headed back in the same direction.

"Was that Lafleur?" Colby asked, grabbing the dashboard.

"Probably not. Most likely someone he got to help him. That was just a warning. Lafleur likes to play like that. He wants me to sweat, to be looking over my shoulder all the time. Then when he thinks I'm sufficiently terrorized, he'll make his move, but it will be dramatic. He's waited too long to shoot me from a car window. He plans to enjoy this."

"How do you know all that?"

"I make it a point to know my enemies." I slowed down, glancing every few seconds in the rearview mirror. "Just before I fought Lafleur that night, a guy walked in and took me aside. He told me I was nuts for fighting Lafleur. I remember him calling me a kid. He told me all the reasons I would lose. Lafleur was older, heavier, and he'd been fighting for years."

"Weren't you scared?"

"I was terrified, but I knew that fear wasn't going to help me stay alive. Anyway, this guy had been friends with Lafleur for many years, but they'd had a falling out. He told me that my only chance to beat Lafleur was to understand what made him tick, to cause him to lose his concentration."

"So you used psychology on Lafleur to win?"

"With what Art told me, I was able to distract him by making him react to comments about his ex-wife, whom he still loves. Apparently, she'd cheated on him several times, and I tormented him with that fact. He was surprised that I knew that stuff and it made him hesitate when he responded. Often, I'd be able to anticipate his next move. When he was wavered, I hit hard, making it count. It weakened him some."

I stopped at a light. "Art told me Lafleur enjoyed giving pain. He didn't believe in ending things quickly, and this gave me time to wear him out. I had one thing going for me. I was younger, and I had a lot of stamina. Lafleur was convinced I'd be an easy win and he let down his guard, started to play with me, showing off for his buddies in the crowd. I was pretty beaten, and getting tired, too. I'd lost a lot of blood. I remember the room spinning. I hit him when he wasn't looking, went for the eyes. I figured if he couldn't see me, he couldn't kill me."

"You blinded him."

"Yes. Stabbed him through the right eye. He screamed something terrible. I could have killed him then. I hesitated, and that's when he felt around for the metal pipe and got me across the knees."

Colby sighed. "Things would have been so different if he hadn't done that."

"Yeah. I might have had a career. I was good. I was real good."

I glanced again in my mirror and took the next exit. The safe house was in a secluded area that very few people knew about. I hoped I wouldn't have to explain to Colby why I'd built this place so deep in the woods, but he'd probably figure it out once he saw it. I'd brought many men to that cabin, men who wanted only one thing. Since Colby, I hadn't used it. Now it was proving to be handy for something else indeed.

When I turned onto a dirt road, Colby said, "Holy shit, you weren't kidding when you told me this place was remote. What the hell are we supposed to do out here, hunt rabbits?"

I smiled. "You'll be fine. There is a lot of food, and I'll have someone bring you more if you run out. Hopefully, I'll be able to take care of things fast, and this will all be over. Then we can go and get your kids."

He raised an eyebrow. "And if Lafleur kills you?"

"Don't worry. I've made sure you will be all right if something happens to me. Someone will come and—Lafleur won't hunt you anymore."

"Damn it, Diego. Why are you such an asshole?"

I glanced at him.

"I'm worried about you."

"I'll be okay."

He didn't get out of the van as I came to a stop.

"What is it now?"

"I can't raise two kids like this."

I looked straight ahead. "If at any time you want out, I'll make it happen."

"And you?" He met my gaze.

"Colby, damn it, not this now."

"When then?"

"I don't know. I'll help you with the kids. I'll give you money, set you up some place far from here and—"

"And what? I'll meet the boy next door, get married, and live happily ever after?"

"Maybe you will," I muttered.

Colby reached out and grabbed my vest. He pulled me closer. "I don't want the fucking boy next door." He met my gaze. "I only want you." He released me, glancing at the cabin. "So, if you fuck me here, how many will that make on the bedpost?"

"What?"

"Don't play coy with me, Diego." He opened the door and got out.

Here we go. I got out after him.

Thankfully the door opened, and Nuts came out. "Ahoy there, mates!"

Colby just brushed by him and walked inside.

"He's in a mood. What's with him?" Nuts asked.

"It's been tough." I ran a hand through my hair.

"Oh yeah, that. You look like hell."

"Gee thanks, Nuts," I told him. "I need a shower and something to eat. Did one of the prospects drive my bike up here?"

"It's in the back. Yeah. And now it's just me and Marcel here like you said. He's out back chopping wood for the fireplace."

"Good. How is Cherise?"

"Being Cherise. Lots of questions about Lafleur." He pulled out a cigarette.

I looked at him. "My mom has cancer." I grabbed the cigarette and threw it away.

He frowned. "Sorry, man."

"How much doesn't she know about this anyway? I told you not to talk about it."

"She knows his name, knows someone is after you. That's all. Hear from Chase?"

I wasn't happy that Nuts had such a big mouth. "No."

"He called. Wanted to know where you were at. Is he coming up here?"

"No. You and Marcel only for now. Okay?"

He nodded.

I walked into the cabin. Nuts followed me.

I looked around and smiled faintly. I'd built most of this place by myself. One big open space for the kitchen and living room, with three bedrooms and a bathroom. I'd even put in a standing shower and a hot tub. I'd made history in that hot tub, but that was my secret.

On the other side, looking out over the woods was a beautiful porch made from cedar that went all the way around the house.

The balcony door was open. I could see Cherise sitting out there in a winged chair. Colby was perched on the railing in front of her, stroking his dog. They looked deep in conversation. I changed my mind about interrupting them.

Instead, I told Nuts I was going to take a shower.

"I did what you told me boss, and had Tammy go out and buy some clothes for you all."

"Good."

"You're in the room on the end. I put Colby next to you. Cherise is in the room on the other end. Marcel and I will take turns on watch and on the sofa."

"Good."

"That thing sleeps better than the bed," he said. "Posto back or something like that." He patted the sofa.

"You mean, Posturepedic, it's a brand."

"Yeah, that's the one."

I shook my head, grinned and walked into the bathroom. I took off my clothes and pulled the elastic out of my hair, then opened the round glass shower door. I closed it and stepped inside, happy to see shower gel and some aromatic shampoo. I adjusted the taps to a nice warm temperature, stood under the spray, and squirted some shampoo in my hand and began to rub it over my head. I hadn't realized how long my hair was until I began to rinse out the soap. It was well past my shoulders. Next, I pumped out some shower gel and rubbed my hands over my chest, my arms, moving down to my cock, which I took in hand. I closed my eyes, stroking it a little. I was hard thinking that maybe I'd get the chance to fuck Colby in this shower. But with everyone around, maybe not. I kept stroking, my tongue licking the water from my bottom lip.

"*Come for me, Diego. Come.*" I saw Colby in my mind's eye, watching me, urging me on. He stroked his own erection while I did the same. My back hit the tiles, and I moaned softly, my chest heaving as the water rinsed the come through my fingers.

"Um, baby, that's the most erotic thing I've ever seen."

My eyes snapped open as the door to the shower opened. Colby stood there naked.

"What are you doing in here?" I demanded in a hushed whisper, taking my hand off my cock.

"Well," he said softly as he made no pretense that he was examining every inch of me. "I tried the door and . . . you left it open. I didn't know you were in the . . . well . . ." He smiled. "Maybe I did. It's locked now."

"What?" I breathed.

"The door," he said, coming in and closing the shower.

"What are you doing?"

"What does it look like I'm doing?"

"Are you . . . insane?" I made a move to come out of the

shower as he moved in closer.

He put a hand on my chest and pushed me back. "Yeah." He nodded. "I'm insane. Or maybe I just need a shower." He met my gaze, then pressed me against the wall. "Why are you breathing so hard?" He was looking at my chest as he grabbed my wrists and lifted them, holding me against the tiles.

"Am I?" I asked.

"Um, yeah." While holding my arms against the tiles, he licked my chest, then moved his tongue over one of my nipples. He looked up at me, his erection slapping my thigh. "Do me a favor?"

"Ah, okay," I said as his cock slapped me again. I could hardly get the breath into my lungs.

"Keep your arms like that. You are turning me on big time so . . . but I do need my hands quite desperately at the moment."

"To do what with?" I tried to look innocent.

He bit his bottom lip. "Shall I tell you?"

"If you want to." My head moved to the side as he kissed my neck.

"Promise you won't lower your hands?"

"I promise."

"And you'll spread your legs a little wider?"

"All right."

"And you'll do whatever I tell you to?"

"Um, that depends."

"On what?"

"On what I get in return." I was so ready to fuck him, but he wanted to play with me. He planned to make me wait.

"What do you want?" It was his turn to act coy.

"I want to fuck you." I looked into those eyes. "I want to fuck you, Colby." That came out sounding like a moan.

His chest was heaving now. "We'll see," he whispered.

"There might be a struggle."

I smiled. "I can handle that."

He lifted his head. "You're an arrogant one. Too good-looking, that's your problem. Some guys . . . well . . . they might go for the strong, macho types with killer eyes . . . that mix of Latin . . . that makes the blood boil hot." Colby flicked a tongue across my nipple again, a hand trailed down my chest. I felt his fingertips dance down the length of my cock. I grunted.

"Very sensitive." He moved a finger over my lips, then pressed his mouth there. He kissed me hot and rough, caressing my tongue with his as one hand wrapped around my erection. He stroked me so sweetly I almost came, but he knew when to stop. He knew my body almost as well as I knew it. He knew how to make me last. It didn't matter if I was fucking him, he was always in control. He would have me when he was ready and not before that.

Colby moved back. His hand grasped my balls and fondled them lightly. A soft cuff against my cock and I let my head go back. "Turn around," he said. "Keep your hands up."

"Making me practice for arrest?"

"Don't joke about that, and I didn't tell you to speak."

"Okay." I smiled.

He nudged my legs apart. "God, you're beautiful." His hands slid over my shoulders and down my back to my waist. He cupped my ass cheeks and gently squeezed as he moved his cock against me. Um. That was nice.

A little smack made me laugh. He was the only one in the world who would ever dare do that to me. He reached under me and lightly touched my balls while his other hand spread my cheeks. I felt a soapy finger enter me. I jolted, didn't expect it. He pulled my hair back and turned my head for a kiss as he went deeper with his finger. He let go and pressed me flat again. He was on his knees now. The finger was gone, and he began to rim me with his tongue. My hands went into fists. Each time I moved, he told me to stay still. My cock was aching.

He stood and told me turn around again. He let his gaze trail over me again. "Oh yeah, your cock is perfect. So hard." He gave it a tug, and a few slaps. My cock reacted. He stood there looking at me.

"Colby," I moaned.

"Yes, baby." He pressed on my shoulder. "Get down on your knees."

I went down on my haunches, the water still running on me. Colby pushed back my head and moved in. He let his erection brush my lips. "Open your mouth and suck it. Come on," he gritted out. "Eat it."

I opened my mouth and took in as much as I could. His cock was slick with pre-come. It wouldn't take much. He was really turned on. It pleased me that I could get him so hot. He grabbed my hair and pushed in deeper, his thumbs caressing my face. I almost fell over backwards. I reached out a hand to steady myself, and pushed up and down, my entire body moving as I blew him.

When he came, it was like watching the dirtiest gay porn. Only this wasn't fake. This was real, and it was beautiful. I had to fight not to come as I watched him. But I had plans for my erection. He pulled back as he was coming, but I'd swallowed some. He hit the wall, his hand on his cock. He put his mouth against his arm to muffle his cries.

I stood. Our gazes met and locked. He knew what was next. "Your ass is mine," I told him.

He grinned. "What if I say no?"

A little game he wanted to play. I knew he wasn't saying no. He wanted it rough. He wanted to play with me, and I was wound up enough. I remembered Colby telling me once

that he'd never met a man who could really handle him . . .
his sexual appetite could run on the wild side. But given that
he kept coming back for more, I figured I was doing okay.

I tilted my head, looked at him. "You don't want me to
fuck you then?"

"No. I'm not hard anymore. I've had what I wanted from
you." On his face was the challenge. Ooh. I liked it. I liked it
a lot.

"Well, that's too bad," I said, roughly pressing him
against the tile, "because right now, I want your ass. And I
intend to have it."

I took his sex in my hand and lifted it. I stroked it in my
palm and heard his breathing quicken. He let his head fall
back against the wall, and he closed his eyes.

"Um, surrender?" I suggested, squeezing his balls and letting my tongue explore his chest.

"Never," he grunted.

I licked and tongued his nipples, while I stroked his cock
and alternately handled his balls. He was hard again, pant-
ing, trying to hump my leg. I moved back. "Now, either turn
against the wall or I'll turn you."

He licked his lips. "If you want me, then take me. But I
won't surrender."

I tried not to smile. He wanted the big, tough gang leader.
I didn't kiss him although I wanted to. Instead, I moved him
around to face the wall.

"Am I your prisoner?" he whispered.

"Oh yeah, baby," I told him. "Prisoner of love."

I heard his soft chuckle. "Condom is on the soap tray."

"For an unwilling victim, you do come prepared."

"Shut up."

I kissed his neck and inserted a soapy finger in his ass. He
grunted. "What did you say?"

"Nothing."

"You sure?" I put two up there and finger fucked him. I checked his cock again. Oh, he was ready. He was humping my fingers.

"You'll pay for this," he whispered.

"I hope so," I told him. I pulled out my fingers and slipped on the condom. "Guess you're not helping me put on the rubber eh?"

"Fuck yourself, you hood."

I smiled. "Okay, but I'd rather . . ." I positioned my cock at his entrance. "Fuck you." I pushed up into his ass, and he made an attempt to struggle free. I held him against the wall. "You surrender now?" I pushed in deeper.

He moaned. "Oh . . . God . . . Fuck . . . Diego. Yeah. Yeah . . . whatever. Fuck me. Fuck me. I love your cock."

I didn't answer. In fact, we didn't talk for some time after that moment. All games had been played. Now there was just me and Colby, fucking like two crazy men, trying not to make any noise. Not easy.

When it was over, and I pulled my cock out of him, Colby turned in my arms and held me so tight, I wondered if he'd ever let go. He ran his hands over my back, then reached over and adjusted the water, made it warmer. "Let me wash you."

"You'll make me hard again."

He looked up into my eyes. "So, you'll have to fuck me again."

"Colby." I shook my head. "They're going to wonder what in hell we're doing in here."

"We're talking. Working out stuff."

"I guess." I smiled.

He ran the soap over my chest, then touched the scar on top of my right bicep. "Are those magic stitches?" he asked.

"Not sure how magic they are," I teased.

"I mean, do they disappear?"

"Yes."

"Does it hurt?" He put his lips there.

"No, but my cock is beginning to."

"Yeah?" He ran his soapy hand over my cock.

"Colby," I grunted.

"You're hard again. You seem to have a real problem with that."

"I do, do I?" I grabbed him and tickled him. He laughed and struggled away.

"I think you should wash yourself," he said. "You have no self-control."

I made a face and pointed to his erection. "Only me?" I lifted an eyebrow.

"If you did it, then take care of it."

"Colby, stop it. I can't. We have to get out of here. I need to go."

Colby wrapped his arms around me. "I don't want you to go. I don't want you to go after Lafleur. Let's just leave. You and me. The kids. Your mom and the dog. Please. We'll just drive and never look back."

I pushed some of his wet hair back. "I'm sorry, baby. I can't."

He stepped away from me. "You're full of shit. You like fucking me, but you don't really love me."

"Colby." I sighed.

He opened the shower door. I turned off the water. "If you loved me, you'd leave here with me today. You love that stupid vest more."

I grabbed the towel and got out. "Is that what you think?"

"Yeah, that's what I think." He looked at the hot tub. "So, how many men were lucky enough to get fucked by you in there?"

"Long time ago."

"Not so long." He met my gaze. "Anyway, don't worry

about your stupid reputation as a lady's man," Colby said on the way out. "I'll say I was in the hot tub while you were in the shower, just two good ol' boys shooting the breeze."

I sighed. The door closed.

After I'd dried off and gone to the room to change, I came out into the living room to see my mother sitting on the sofa. When she saw me, she said, "About time you make an appearance. You didn't drown in there, did you?"

Colby was making toast in the kitchen. He didn't say anything. Nuts was watching some black and white movie on television. I could hear the chopping sound coming from out back again, so I knew where Marcel was.

I leaned down to kiss her cheek. She looked haggard. "I guess I just needed a little time."

She rubbed the stubble on my jaw. "In my day, men actually shaved smooth. What is it with all that rough jaw business anyway? And that hair, Diego. It is way too long."

I'd lost the elastic.

"Anything else?" I grinned and sat beside her.

She slapped me on the arm.

"How are you feeling?"

"I've started the treatments. Just one so far, but I feel okay." She took my hand. She glanced at Colby, and I knew she felt anxious about him, but instead, she said, "I'm worried about the house, Diego."

"I told you not to worry about anything. The prospects are watching it. No one would dare touch that house, Mama. It's under Banni protection."

"The Banni, Banni." She shook her head. "A goddamn necessary evil." She squeezed my hand. "Now, you tell me what's going on. Who wants to hurt my boy this time?"

I smiled at her. "Want something to eat?"

"Don't change the subject, Diego. You think that smile of yours is going to distract me. I'm your mama. I know you.

Your daddy had the same smile. That smile is the reason you is here."

"I don't want to hear about him," I said.

"You have no call to hate your daddy, child. He the one who helped to make you. Can't help that. And look at you, fine looking man. Colby, Nuts, you ever seen a finer looking man than my Diego?"

"No, Mama," Nuts called out. "If I was a girl, I'd be all over him."

I made a face at him.

Mama looked at Colby. "Haven't heard from you yet."

"Leave him alone, Mama."

Colby came over with his toast and kissed my mother's face. "He's got some of your looks, too."

"Yeah." She nodded. "Got my eyes, my temper, but he's his daddy all over."

I sighed softly. If she hadn't been sick, I would have gotten angry. But I held my tongue.

"That man was fine, Colby. Every girl in town be wanting to get with him. He was charming, too. All his fancy talk. And so tall, broad-shouldered, all muscle. I'm telling you there wasn't a man for miles round that would have messed with him."

I stood. "Going to get some air."

"You stay here." Mama grabbed my arm. "Listen to what I'm going to tell you. If something happens to me, I don't want you to be alone."

"Nothing is going to happen, Mama." I touched her shoulder.

"Hush, child," she said. "Sit still."

I sighed and relaxed back on the sofa.

"I know where your father is."

My eyes widened.

"I didn't tell you before 'cause I knew you'd get all

worked up about it."

"Doesn't matter," I said. "I don't want to know where he is."

"He called me not too long ago."

"What?" I was stunned.

"He heard from one of the neighbors I was sick. He called to see if I was dead yet." She laughed aloud.

"Why didn't you hang up?" I snapped.

"Why in the world would I hang up? He called because you're his baby. Just like you're mine. And I got no God-given right to keep a father from his own flesh and blood."

"You're not keeping me from him. I want nothing to do with the bastard."

Nuts stood up. "Think I'll check outside."

"I'll go with you." Colby jumped up.

Cherise shook her head. "Colby, you stay."

Colby sat back down as Nuts left. "Okay."

She reached out and took his hand, then took mine. She pulled our hands together on her lap. We were both looking at her. "Your father went to prison a few years after you were born, Diego. I didn't want you to know, but that's why he wasn't there for you."

Why in hell was she telling me all this now? "Mama, please don't."

"You gotta hear this now in case something happens to me."

"Nothing is going to—"

"Hush, boy."

"Okay, what did he do?"

"He was accused of sexually assaulting the wife of a prominent businessman in town."

"Sexual assault? Oh my God." Could it get any worse?

"But he didn't do it." She looked at me. "I know 'cause the woman told me after your daddy was arrested. I tried to tell the authorities, but she be a white woman with money. They didn't listen to anything I had to say. He did ten years. When he came out, he was a broken man. He changed his name and took up the boxing trade, fighting across the county. That witch, she died two years after your daddy was released. She was sick and dying, and on her deathbed, she admitted she'd lied. Your daddy never touched her. It was just wishful thinking on her part."

I was speechless.

"Say something."

"Why didn't you tell me this?"

"He asked me not to. When he came out, he still had a record. He thought it would hurt you knowing your daddy was a convicted rapist. When he was cleared, it was too late. You were almost a man. He said he wouldn't know what to say to you."

"And now what?"

"He didn't tell me to tell you this. I wanted to. I want to see the two men that mean the most to me in the same room before I die. I'm afraid." She squeezed both our hands. "Colby?" She looked at him. "Please, you love my boy. Don't let anything happen to him."

Colby drew back. "Cherise, there's nothing I can do." He looked at me.

I sighed. "Mama, did you tell anyone these things . . . about Colby and me?"

"Of course not."

"Just asking."

"Listen to me, I know one thing," she said. "The two of you will never have a life together if you don't get away from here and away from the Banni."

"Mama, it's not that simple." I stood. "I can't talk about this now."

"Fine. Then talk to me about this maniac you blinded a

few years back?"

I sighed. "Damn it. Who told you I'd blinded him?"

"I keep my ears open. I know what happened in that fight. People talk. Said you almost died. They say this Lafleur is a tough mother, been in the prison, done hard time."

I leaned down and kissed her cheek. "It will be okay, Mama."

"And about those two children." She looked at Colby. "Do you think Cledus and June know yet that the law is after them?"

He shrugged. "I don't know. And the not knowing is driving me insane."

She rocked back and forth a bit. "When this is over, when you're safe again, you go get those kids, and you love them, and protect them. Get away from all this . . . violence."

Colby nodded. He was emotional. I could see it in his face. I didn't expect him to say anything, but he did. "I love those kids, and I'm going to take care of them. But . . ." He looked at me. "I could never leave your son. I love him too much."

Our gazes met and locked. Then I looked away, clearing my throat. "I have to go."

My mother struggled to her feet as I headed to the door. "Diego!"

I turned and faced her. Colby had come to support her.

"Rest, Mama. Get well. I love you." I looked at Colby. "I'll try to fix this fast so you can get the kids."

I walked outside. I heard my mother cry out my name again.

I looked at Nuts. "Don't tell them anything more," I grunted.

"What do you mean?"

"Just don't talk to Mama or Colby about Lafleur again,

okay?"

"Okay." He spat out a nutshell right next to my foot. It was huge. It looked like a dead roach. I sure hoped it wasn't. "Is everything all right?"

I sighed. "I gotta go. Where's my bike?"

"Around back."

I walked over to see my bike and the passenger van Nuts had come out here with. I waved to Marcel in the distance. He'd stopped chopping and was arranging wood in bundles. I got on the bike, started the engine, hit the gas, then roared off down the road. I didn't look back to see if anyone was looking.

CHAPTER SIX

I didn't go to the clubhouse. Instead, I drove back into the city and stopped downtown at a little eatery I liked to have a hamburger and a beer. The food was good, but I didn't have much of an appetite. I paid and tipped the waitress, then pressed the speed dial for Chase on the way out. I was checking out anyone who looked twice at me, imagining that there was a gun under everyone's jacket. It was insane.

Chase picked up on the third ring.

"Where are you?" I asked.

"Babysitting your cop, B.S. It's my new nickname for him."

Bradley Simpson. It fit I guess. "How is he?"

"Dry and pissed off, like I usually get when I don't have a drink. Your name came up a few times."

"I bet it did."

"So, wanna meet at the clubhouse? I should be with you, watching your back at this time."

"Yeah. But not just yet. Do you know if they picked up Cledus?"

"News is they're looking for his ass."

"Um."

"I know that little um. Whatcha thinking?"

"I'll let you know."

"What do you want us to do with sourpuss?"

"If he's ready, turn him loose."

"Done."

I hung up. I knew that Cledus and Gilles Lafleur were

about the same age. They hadn't been in the same club, but I was sure they'd run in some of the same circles at one time. Also, Cledus was the only one who might suspect that Colby and I were more than just friends. He'd been doing the nasty himself with another man, and, as they say, takes one to know one. I'd go with my hunch. Cledus was first on my list, after that was Chase, but I really doubted Chase would betray me in that way. He had way too much to lose.

It took me longer than I thought to track down Cledus. I needed to get to that bastard before the police did. I had a feeling that Gilles had given him sanctuary.

Gilles Lafleur had owned an apartment block not far from where I grew up, near the downtown core. When Lafleur went to the joint, he'd transferred it to his aunt, a con woman everyone called Tricky Trudy. She turned the place into a prostitution den. The four-apartment block was near the railroad tracks, hidden away behind an abandoned needle factory. The factory was mainly used now as a drug den where people squatted and shot up.

There was a street gang, a bunch of punks, who called themselves the Killers. They patrolled the area, supplying the junk. The leader, a seventeen-year-old with a bald head and studs in every orifice thought he was just about the toughest son of a bitch who ever lived.

It was after dark when I rode my bike slowly along the tracks and then pulled up alongside the factory's former parking lot. I got off my bike, helmet dangling from one hand, and walked around to the back. I stood looking at the apartment building. At one time, it was probably a nice place. Now, everything was falling apart. The windows were broken, the screens torn. There were holes in the door, and the steps leading to the front door were crumbling.

I saw lights on everywhere, and heavy metal music blared. Around the side of the building, several cars sat parked. It looked like Tricky Trudy was doing good business.

I heard footsteps behind me and turned to see a few of the punks. One of them was the leader. I'd seen him before when I came down here to find Chase. He'd been on one of his drunks, and I'd found him butt-ass naked lying on a table with a piece of celery sticking out of his ass. Not a pretty sight.

That kid, who called himself Vlad, had actually helped me get Chase out of there, but that had been two years ago. Vlad had aged and not in a good way. He sneered at me. I'd taken off my vest and shoved it in my locker on the back of the bike. I figured it made me less of a target.

"What do we have here?" Vlad sneered. "Lookin' to get high, laid, or both?"

"Neither actually," I said. "I'm looking for someone." I walked over to him.

He watched me, sizing me up, wondering if he could take me. I was at least sixty pounds heavier and six inches taller. "What, do I look like, your mommy?"

I folded my arms across my chest and looked at him. The two punk asses with him were sniggering. "No, actually, you look like a little fuckwad that is just dying to be taught a lesson."

His expression sobered, and he sneered. "You looking for trouble, you found it." He marched up closer. "I'm going to fuck you up."

I laughed. "You can try." I met his gaze.

Something flickered in his. He whipped out a switchblade. My gaze went to the glittering steel, and I sighed. "Really?"

"I'm good."

"Um." I nodded and fixed him with a stare. "Maybe, but I'm better."

He took a step back.

"Now, you can help me find someone, or you can fuck off. You choose."

"This is my territory."

I looked around. "I wouldn't brag if I were you."

"Smartass!" He was going to make a move. Jesus.

He lunged at me. I put out my hand and grabbed the front of his throat. I squeezed, and he went to his knees in front of me, his eyes wide. I heard the knife clatter to the pavement. The other two turned and ran.

I released the pressure and watched him choke, trying to get his breath. In between each cough, he managed to get out, "Who . . . are . . . you?"

I looked down at him, extended my hand and pulled him to his feet. "My name is Diego Champagne."

He stumbled back. "Fuck!"

I put up a hand. "It's over?"

He nodded.

"Fuck man . . . you're the leader of the Banni."

"I am."

"Why in the shit . . . why didn't you say so?"

"You're a smart kid. I thought you'd figure it out."

"So, ah . . . who you looking for, man? What can I do to help you? Say it, anything."

He was suddenly my adoring fan. "Where's your colors?"

"On my bike."

"Can I see? Can I look at your vest, touch it, man?"

"Later. Can you do me a favor?"

"Sure, anything, you name it, man."

"Okay, I want you to go inside." I glanced at the building. "And without calling too much attention to yourself, find out if there's a man in there called Cledus Young."

"Okay. And do you want me to beat him, man?"

"No. I don't want you to do anything. Just come out here

and tell me if he's in there."

He nodded and went running off toward the building. I leaned against the old factory and waited.

Seconds later I felt my phone vibrate in my pocket. I took it out and glanced at it. It was Badger. "Yeah?"

"Hey, you still dead man walkin'?"

"Something like that."

"Any sign of Lafleur?"

"Not yet. I got reason to believe he may have paired up with Cledus Young. He's wanted right now for child abuse. Helped to kill his own kid."

A pause. "You mean Colby's sister? Bastard. We find him, we'll kill him."

"No, I want him alive."

"Whatever, brother."

"So what's up?"

"I got some people ready to do harvesting. You sending down some folks or you want me to take care of it? We got plenty of people willing to work."

"You can trust these people to keep their mouths shut?" My gaze was on the whorehouse.

"They know better than to double-cross the Crushers. In it for the money, some got bigger rap sheets than I do. Some illegal migrant workers. They won't tell no one."

"Make sure they get paid well. If they get paid, they'll be less likely to talk. We'll work it out for the split."

"No sweat, my man. When we going to see each other?"

"Soon as I deal with Lafleur."

"I hear you. Keep the faith," Badger said and rang off.

Where in the hell was that Vlad kid? I was just about to go in there when I saw him come walking out. He ran across to me. I pulled him up against the building. "He's there," he said.

"Keep your voice down. Where is he?" I looked over at

the building again.

"He's on the second floor. See that window where the curtain is blowing out?"

"Yeah."

"He was sleeping in there. Don't know how he can sleep, man. Trudy said he's drunk."

"He alone?"

"Yeah. Now what?"

"Go home," I told him.

"No, man. I wanna help."

I looked at him. "I don't need your help."

"Can I join the Banni?"

"What?"

"I want to join, man. My talents are being wasted here."

I realized that I could do something here, something real, something that might affect this kid's life forever. In spite of everything, I had to.

"Okay," I told him. "You gotta go through initiation first."

He looked at me. "What do I gotta do?"

"The next person who walks out of that building, I want you to kill them."

His eyes widened. "Oh, okay . . . like for nothing?"

"For nothing. Take that blade there and slit their throat." I hoped he wasn't going to call my bluff. He wasn't. He was shitting his pants.

"Can't do it?"

"I can."

"Well, do it then!"

"There's no one coming out yet." He was shaking like a leaf.

"Ever see what someone's head looks like after being shot with an automatic rifle at close range?"

He shook his head.

"What about what's it like to burn a man's tat off his back with a torch?"

He shuddered. "Why you telling me that? The open road, man, the chicks, the parties, and having brothers and —"

"And jail, and mug shots, and people trying to shoot you, and bar fights . . . getting the clap . . . running afoul of the mob, watching people bleed and die."

He looked at me.

"Not being able to live your life the way you want to, or love who you want to . . . to always be under pressure to feel tough even when you don't feel tough."

He fell silent.

I put a hand on his shoulder. "Kid, get your life together, and take that shit out of your lip and your nose, go back to school and be somebody. Don't waste your life like I have . . . you'll die young, and no one will remember your name. Find someone to love and hold on to them forever."

"That shit sounds boring."

"Funny, to me, it sounds like heaven. Now, get out of here."

He walked away, but he didn't disappear. He stood there watching me. I wondered if anything I said penetrated. Well, I didn't have too much time to play social worker. I walked across to the building. Showtime.

The smell of come and urine assaulted my nose as soon as I entered the dirty lobby. The doors of the two apartments downstairs were open, and there was a party going on. I took the staircase, passing two hopelessly drugged-out guys on the way down and turned the corner on the second landing. The door was open there, too. There were a bunch of people singing along drunkenly to some AC/DC song. Good God.

I walked in to see three topless ladies who didn't look a day over sixteen and some dirty old men with too much belly lounging around as the girls danced in front of them.

An older woman walked out of the kitchen; too much makeup and too much hard living made her seem far older than I'm sure she was. She had on a low-cut dressing gown with a push-up bra that was pushing her right out of it, and a cigarette dangling from her lips. She looked at me, narrowing her eyes, probably trying to figure out if I was the heat.

We met in the middle of the living room.

"What can I do you for, honey?" She laughed, choking on her cigarette smoke. "Or can I just do ya? You are one fine specimen of manhood."

You got to be kidding! I lowered my head and spoke beside her ear. "I don't want any trouble. I'll just take what I came for and go."

She glanced up at me as I drew back. "You Banni?"

I glanced toward the bedroom. "Yeah. He in there?"

She hooked her thumb toward the room. "I want no biker problem. That's what I told Gilles, le maudit. I run a clean establishment. Take that shithead and go."

"You won't get any trouble from the Banni if you do me a favor."

"Sure, honey, which one of my beauties you want?" She waved her hand around the room.

"None. I want you to give your nephew a message. You tell him if he wants Diego Champagne, to show up at the scrapyard, tomorrow night at midnight. I'll be there waiting for him, and I'll be alone."

Her eyes widened. "You Champagne?"

I nodded and headed down the hallway. I opened the door. Cledus was there on the bed, snoring. I put my gun to his head. "Wakey, wakey," I told him.

Cledus opened his eyes. He was about to holler as I patted him down. I shook my finger in front of him. "I wouldn't if I were you. Now, if I was you, and I'm not, but just sayin',

I'd be real quiet and just walk out of here nicely with me."

He nodded. I held the gun on him, and he got out of bed. He reeked. I think he'd pissed himself. "I'm not a well man."

"You're going to be a helluva lot less well if you mess with me tonight."

He nodded.

We walked out of the apartment without an issue, got to the stairs, and it was then Cledus decided to be trouble. He gave me a shove, but I grabbed him and took him with me. We went rolling down the stairs together. Shit. That hurt. At the bottom, I shook myself. Cledus scrambled to his feet and took off out the door. This just keeps getting better and better.

I chased after him. I had the advantage. Cledus was old and sick. I was young and healthy, but I had bad knees. I could run fast, but after a little while, my knees would cry out for relief. I was going to pay tomorrow. Luckily that old man couldn't run far, but eventually, he went into the last place I wanted to be—he slipped inside the old factory.

It was dark in there and full of vagrants shooting themselves up with smack. They were sad and dangerous people. I couldn't see a damn thing until my eyes adjusted. I knew there were rats in there. I heard them scurrying around.

Cledus had stopped running. He was hiding in the shadows, but his heavy breathing gave him away.

I stumbled on someone lying on the floor, wrapped in a blanket. Jesus. Were they dead? I reached out in the dark and grabbed Cledus.

"Don't hurt me," he pleaded. "I'm sick. I'm a sick old man."

"Come on." I grunted and pushed him ahead of me. "You run again, I'll shoot you."

"I can't. I'm all used up," he said. Outside he turned to me. "It was Gilles. He paid me."

"He pay you to finger your son, too?"

"I let it slip that Colby was fucking you. It was said in casual conversation."

"Casual conversation? You son of a bitch." I wanted to kick his ass. "Who else knows that?"

"No one, I swear." He was sweating, his hands in the air.

"How did you find out?"

"My son is like me, always had a taste for cock and a taste for guys who can handle him in bed. I took one look at you and knew. Doesn't make you gay you know, if you're always the doer. That's what Gilles said."

I grabbed him by the shirt. "Fuck what Gilles said. You repeat what you just said to anyone, and I'll strip the flesh from your bones, you got me?"

He nodded frantically.

"Now, you're going to tell me where your buddy Gilles is."

"I don't know, Diego, I swear, man. He's out for your blood." He actually smiled. "I'll enjoy watching you die."

"Well, I got news for you. It looks like you're going to miss the show. The cops are looking for you."

He narrowed his eyes. "What for?"

"What for? How about for the murder of your little girl, Garnet Beauty?"

"I . . . I don't know what . . . you're talking about, Diego. I never touched her." He frowned. "Are you saying they found her? Where's she been all this time?"

"As if you didn't know. I should kill you. I really should, but I'll let the law deal with you. It will more fun thinking of you up there in the pen. I'm sure you'll make a lot of friends."

"I don't care." He sighed. "I'm dying anyway. Doc says I may only have a few weeks."

"I don't give a shit," I told him, then hauled off and hit

him in the face. "That's for that little girl you helped murder." I hit him again, this time hard enough to knock him on
his ass. "And that's for Colby."

I looked down at him. He was crying.

"You're one pathetic son of a bitch. Get up."

"So you can hit me again?" He wiped the blood from his
lip.

"No, so you can take me to Lafleur." I pulled him to his
feet.

"He's got a drag queen as an old lady . . . or ladyboy . . .
some such. Like the Crying Game, man, and I don't know
where she, he, it is."

"Well, I'll just have to jog your memory then. Let's go
where we can have a bit more privacy. How did you get
here?"

"In my car."

"Take me to it."

"You won't get away with this." He wiped the blood from
his mouth again. "I'm telling you, Gilles is going to kick
your ass, and I'm going to be there, applauding when he
does."

"No," I told him. "I don't think so."

He led me to a beat-up old Ford out behind the building
in the grown-over parking lot.

I took his keys after he'd opened the door. "Get in behind
the wheel," I told him.

Vlad had followed us. I was actually glad to see him.
"Kid," I called, "come over here."

He came on the run. "What can I do?"

I tossed him the key to my bike. "I want you to take care
of my bike for me. Can you do that?"

"Yes, sir." He nodded. "I'll take really good care of it. I
know just the place to put it."

"Perfect. You got a cell phone?"

"Yeah." He took it out of his pocket. "You want it?"

"No. I want your number so I can call you. I'll send some-one to pick up the bike tomorrow. Can you handle that?"

"Yes, I'll do it. You'll be pleased, man. I won't fuck up. Can I ride it?"

"No. Give me your number."

He walked up to me and handed me a card. It read Vlad. The phone number was written underneath. "I do 'em my-self. I save them to give to hot girls. You want some? I'll do some for you."

"I don't need a calling card." I got into the passenger side and handed Cledus the car keys. "Okay, let's get out of here." I held the gun on my lap.

Vlad went running off to get my bike.

"You trust that kid not to wreck your ride?" Cledus asked.

"I trust that he wouldn't dare. He knows who I am. He wouldn't be that stupid."

"Real tough, aren't we?"

I didn't answer.

"Let me go, and I'll tell you where Gilles and his ladyboy are." He looked at me slyly as we drove over what seemed like a dozen potholes.

"I thought you said you didn't know where he was?"

"I might, I might not."

"Don't play with me, Cledus. I'm not in the mood."

"Where we going anyway?"

"To the clubhouse."

"What for?"

"For a candle-lit supper, what do you think?"

I watched his speed, told him to slow down a few times. We didn't need to be stopped by the cops. He got real quiet as he drove. Unfortunately, it didn't last. "So, you treated my boy right, Diego?" He chuckled and leered at me.

"Keep your mouth closed and drive."

"Do you love him or just his cock?"

I didn't answer.

"Come on, you're practically my son-in-law."

"Really?" I put the gun up under his jaw. "The only thing I am is your executioner. Keep talking. I'd be doing society a favor taking you out. I wouldn't think twice."

"You'd be doing me a favor. I told you, I'm dying."

I lowered the gun, but I was so close to blowing him away at the next stop sign. I had to fight not to. "Listen, if you're not going to tell me where to find Lafleur, then keep your mouth shut."

He listened that time. A half hour later, we were at the clubhouse. There were several bikes lined up outside. Chase walked outside as soon as we drove up.

I got out and walked around to the driver's side.

Chase came to meet me.

I pointed to Cledus. "Take that piece of shit downstairs and tie him up."

Chase nodded and opened the car door. He practically had to drag Cledus out of the car. He struggled as Chase pulled him across the yard. "You can't do this, Champagne," Cledus bellowed at me.

"Be grateful I'm not putting you in a cage like you did to your daughter." I spit on the ground.

Chase took him inside. I walked in shortly after.

"What do you want us to do with him?" Chase asked as a couple of other members took him away.

"Just tie him up and leave him in the dark. Let him stew for a while about what I'm going to do to him."

"Gotcha."

I had a headache. My knees hurt and I was bruised from rolling down the stairs. But I finally felt as if I had a bit of control over things. I greeted the others and then told them I needed some time by myself. I walked into our meeting room, closed the door, and slumped in my chair. If I couldn't get Cledus to tell me where Gilles was, I'd have to wait until tomorrow night. Hopefully, he'd show up at the scrapyard, and I'd finish this. Then I'd find out what Colby wanted me to do with his father. I'd let him decide.

My cell phone was vibrating. I took it out of my pocket and checked the name. It was Colby. I put the phone to my ear. "I was just thinking about you," I said.

"Is that so?"

"Yeah. How's Mama?"

"Sleeping."

"That's what you should be doing. It's one in the morning."

"Why aren't you sleeping?"

"Got better things to do."

"Are you all right?"

"I guess. I fell down some stairs, but besides that, I guess I'll live."

"You fell down some stairs? What are you, drunk?"

"No. I wish. Colby?"

"What?"

"I have something I want to tell you."

"You love me?" His voice was soft and seductive. It sent a little shiver through me.

"Yes," I said. "I love you."

"Say it again."

"I love you."

"How come it's so easy getting that out of you tonight? That worries me. You find Lafleur?"

"No. But I made sure he can find me."

There was silence.

"Colby?"

"Right. What did you want to tell me?"

"Your father knows about us. He told Lafleur."

"Oh . . . God. Damn him. I want to . . . murder him. How did he know?"

"I'm not sure. He guessed."

"Does anyone else know besides my father and this Lafleur guy?"

"I don't know. Listen. I have him. I have your father. He's here with us."

"You have him. That bastard. That son of . . ."

"Colby. Listen to me. I'm trying to get him to tell me where Lafleur is. When this is over, there are two choices, you can let the police have him or allow the Banni to take care of him. It's your call."

"Thank you for that. Did I ever tell you how much I love you?"

"Tell me again."

"I love you so much. I never thought I'd love someone so much it hurts. But loving you hurts, Diego."

"I'm sorry. It shouldn't."

"No. It shouldn't. When is it, you and Lafleur?"

"If I don't get Cledus to spill his guts, it's tomorrow night at the scrapyard, if he shows up."

"I want to be there."

"You can't. It will distract me. I can't have any distractions. I have to worry about me, not you. Please, don't."

"Okay, but can you take him?"

"I've got to believe I can. He's aged. He's been in prison. It wears a guy down. If he takes me out, it's because his hatred for me is stronger than he is."

"I'll take care of your mom. Don't worry about that, okay?"

"Okay."

"I wish I was there with you. I want so much to hold you, just hold you."

"You will."

"You promise? Promise me, Diego."

"Okay. I promise. Sleep now. Dream about me," I told him and hung up.

I dozed in the chair for a while. I wanted a drink, but I knew I'd have to keep a clear head. When I opened my eyes, it was still dark. I checked my watch. It was four in the morning.

I opened the door to the meeting room and went downstairs. Three of my guys were sitting around playing poker. Chase was one of them. Cledus was sitting in a chair, trussed up like a Christmas turkey. He snarled when he saw me.

"Hello, Cledus," I said. "Time to take that Death Proof tattoo off your back. That club doesn't even exist anymore."

His eyes widened. "You wouldn't dare."

"No?" I leaned down and looked into his face. "Let's see." I looked at Chase. "String him up and get me the blow torch."

Cledus was screaming, and I hadn't even touched him. "What do you want? What do you want? I don't know anything. Fuck!"

I stood there with the blow torch while the guys strung him up. I wasn't really going to do it. Not because he didn't deserve it but because he was dying anyway. I doubt he could have taken too much. I didn't want to kill him. It was for Colby to decide that.

"Where is Gilles Lafleur?" I moved the torch close enough for him to feel the heat. He squealed like a baby. Not more than ten minutes later I had the name and address of Gilles' girlfriend, whom Cledus kept rudely referring to as a 'ladyboy.'

"I gotta piss," he groaned. "I gotta piss."

"Cut him down," I told the boys. "Someone take him to the john." I pressed the speed dial for Colby. It was early morning. I figured that I'd wake him, but I had to know what he wanted us to do with his old man.

I was surprised when he picked up right away. "Diego? Are you all right?"

"I'm fine. Why aren't you asleep?"

"'Cause I'm talking to you."

"Funny. You know what I mean."

"Who can sleep?"

"Your father gave me what I needed. It gives me the element of surprise. I'm going to him."

"Right now?"

"Yeah, it's as good a time as any. Listen, what do you want done with the old man?"

"I want to talk to him on the phone. Lock him in one of the rooms, put a guard outside. I need for him to be alone. I need answers."

"Fair enough. And then what?"

"Then I'll decide if I want him to stand trial or not."

"He's not going to."

"What do you mean?"

I looked over at Cledus, who'd just returned from the bathroom. "He's in bad shape, Colby. He should be in the hospital. Doctors say he doesn't have very long. He's never going to make it to prison."

There was silence.

"Colby?"

"I don't give a damn anyway. He's going to give me his confession before he's in the ground. I need to know why."

"I understand."

"And then . . ." He paused. "And then, turn him over to the police. He'll probably die in a prison hospital awaiting trial, and that's okay 'cause I never want to see him again. Any idea where Calvin is? He's the one who, um, you know, dumped Garnet's body. He's disappeared."

"I'll have Chase look for him. I'll call you as soon as everything is all over, then we'll see if we can get your nephew and niece."

"The cops haven't caught up with my sister, June Gold, yet. I expect to hear from her husband as soon as they do. I love you." He sounded as if he was choking.

"Okay," I said. "You okay?"

"Diego?"

"What?"

"Don't die. Please, don't die."

"I'll do my best not to." I hung up.

Chase looked at me. "I'm coming with you."

I shook my head. "I need to do this alone. You know that."

"Why? Let's just find the bastard and shoot him."

"There's no honor in that."

"Fuck honor."

I smiled. "Not this time." I gave him the instructions concerning Cledus. "Tie him up if you want but leave a hand free and a phone nearby. Colby needs to talk to his old man in private before we give him over to the cops."

"We're going to hand him over?" Chase made a face. He didn't approve.

I nodded. "It's what Colby wants. And there's another thing. We need to find Calvin. He was involved, too. He drove Garnet Beauty into Alabama and abandoned her body in some woods." I paused. "In a water cooler."

A ton of emotions crossed his face. "Okay. I'll put the word out." He shook his head. "I knew Cledus was an ass, but I never thought he . . . well . . . could kill his own kid. Jeez. And Calvin's involved, too . . ."

"Takes all kinds." I reached in my pocket and handed him Vlad's card.

He scanned it. "What in the hell is a Vlad?"

"The leader of some little street gang. He has my bike for safekeeping. Give him a call and find out what he did with it. Send someone to get it, okay?" I took a few hundreds out of my wallet. "And give Vlad this as thanks."

Chase nodded and followed me outside. The sun was up in the sky. It was going to be a hot one. "Hey, I know we've had our differences," Chase said, "but don't get killed, okay?"

"Where have I heard that before?" I grinned. "I'm touched," I added. "Oh, and I'm going to need to borrow your ride."

He threw me the keys. I straddled his bike and roared the motor to life. The other guys came outside to see me off. They knew what was up. I lifted a hand. "If I don't come back, have one hell of a party on me okay?"

CHAPTER SEVEN

Colby

I am not a particularly spiritual man. I am Christian, but I am reluctant to describe myself as such when countless so-called Christians are the most bigoted, hypocritical people I know. But I do believe in God, even when I don't believe in Him if you know what I mean. If there is a God, why does he allow terrible things to happen to children and animals? And while we're on the subject, old people? Why do serial killers and pedophiles thrive but tiny children deal with horrendous illnesses?

And why are polio and measles, two long-eradicated diseases, now all of a sudden a worldwide epidemic, particularly affecting children?

My God, the one I struggle to hold on to, doesn't let these things happen. He's a mighty warrior. Part Thor, part handsome angel, and one hundred percent amazing.

He smites assholes right there in their shoes, nothing but the smoky remains of their socks remaining. It's an image that gives me great satisfaction.

There's an old jazz and blues station here in Baton Rouge that I like to listen to. It's almost surreal that certain songs come on and I know they're meant for me. They speak to me, giving me messages from the sky. Right now, Memphis Minnie was singing, and though I loved her and her song, it didn't hold any special significance for me.

It was early morning, and I was sitting at the kitchen table listening to Cherise's radio in the kitchen. Apart from my dog, she'd brought the radio, a juicer, and a ton of vegetables and fruit when she went into hiding. She also had a laptop that got spotty WiFi we cribbed from some place called Bill Briggs Farms.

Though it was still dark, and dawn wasn't even a suggestion, neither of us could sleep. Beauty lay on the floor at my feet, trying to stay awake, but sleep claimed her. Occasionally she'd open one eye to check on me and Cherise, making sure we were doing okay.

Cherise stood at the sink juicing a boatload of leafy green vegetables. I hate kale, and, apparently, so does Cherise, but according to the Internet, it's a superfood. She shoved it into the whining machine with spinach, grapes, and a few other green things and out spat a thick, green liquid that tasted pretty darn good when she brought me a glass.

"When a person gets sick or gets close to dying," Cherise suddenly said, taking a seat opposite me, "they get religious real quick." It was as though she'd read my mind.

I nodded. "Greens are the best thing you can do for yourself." I pointed to the computer. "It counteracts the drugs, supports your immune system."

She sipped her juice. "This is better without the beets." She shook her head, and I almost cringed. She'd made a batch of juice for us all the night before and, all zealous over her new health regime, she'd taken some bad advice from the Internet and put a lot of raw beetroot into the mix. It had given her, me, Nuts, and poor Marcel stomachaches for hours.

Too late, she'd read that though extremely potent, raw beets are hard to take at first. Small portions are recommended. Marcel and Nuts were in the living room. Their moaning had stopped. I could hear somebody snoring but didn't get up to check which one.

Cherise lit up a small pipe packed with ganja. I couldn't object since it was for medicinal purposes. And it's a green, leafy substance. But what if the cops suddenly showed up with the kids and the place reeked of dope?

Once again, she seemed to be reading my thoughts. She exhaled a thin stream of smoke, tamped down the smoldering grass with a small metal baton and put the pipe away in a vintage metal cigar box she stashed in her overflowing purse.

"When the kids are here, I'll smoke outside," she said, opening the window.

I tensed up again, expecting a call any moment from my sister's husband, Judd. I knew he'd flip out when the cops came for June Gold. He'd huff, and he'd puff that she couldn't have had a hand in any murder, but I knew. I'd been given evidence. I had also seen her be a bitch from hell to my niece, Garnet, named for our sister, and even little Henry. They were so young, Garnet just four and a half, and Henry almost three. I worried about those kids a lot.

A new song came on the radio. 'Autumn Leaves.' I almost wept on the spot. It was the song I felt Garnet Beauty kept sending me from beyond the grave.

Eva sang about lips, summer kisses, and holding sunburned hands. My God. It was even the same version of the song I associated with Garnet.

"Oh, Lord," Cherise said, her eyes welling up. "That's her song." She looked at me, her face stricken. "I think they just arrested June."

We stared at one another. I concentrated on breathing. How did she know about my messages from Heaven? Were Cherise and I that connected?

Cherise broke eye contact first. She dashed from the table and began lighting incense, waving it around the kitchen.

Beauty opened both her eyes and, for some inexplicable

reason, Cherise began chopping some red apples, giving Beauty a couple of quarters. My dog inhaled them as my cell phone rang.

Judd.

"Holy shit," he said, by way of a greeting. Before I could even think of a suitable response, he went on. "Colby, the pigs were just here. They arrested your sister."

Pigs. I'd never heard Judd use language like that before.

"You there?" he snapped.

"I'm here." I waited for him to rail at how unfair and crazy it was for them to apprehend June Gold.

"Did you hear what I said?" His voice got louder and angrier.

"Yeah. I heard."

In the background, Eva sang about missing her darling when the autumn leaves started to fall.

All these years I'd looked after June and even Judd. I'd given them money, and I'd loved their kids like my own. I was about to say something when he said, "They arrested her for the murder of Garnet Beauty."

"I know." It took everything in me not to say; *They sure took their time.*

He went on. I had no idea if he'd even heard me. "That wasn't a murder. It was a mercy killing!" he shrieked.

I couldn't believe what he said. "Don't, Judd. Stop. I don't want to hear this." I thought I'd fall apart, break into a million tiny pieces. The world was going crazy. Spinning in mirrors and shattered glass. My blood seemed to go dry in my veins.

Stop the merry-go-round. I want to get off.

"No. You're right. Not a mercy killing." His voice trembled. "I misspoke. She told me about it years ago. I told her she should have told you everything then. It was a accident."

A accident? He couldn't even speak proper English, and this buffoon was raising two kids.

"An accident?" I cut right through his rambling. "What, she accidently starved her, abused her, choked, and suffocated her?"

He made a choking sound. "She tried to help that little girl. She loved her."

I closed my eyes and held my breath. It had just hit me that he'd known. All this time, all these years, he'd known the truth about Garnet Beauty. The only one who hadn't known was the only one among us who truly loved her. Me. It frightened the heck out of me to think that this jerk of a guy would be responsible for my niece and nephew. That he would be raising them with his attitudes. What if something happened to them? What if they disappeared and all he could say was it was *a accident*?

"She shoulda told you," he said. "Then you woulda known, and you'd never have gone off on this wild goose chase."

"Wild goose chase?" I wanted them to both get arrested. "We found her, Judd. Garnet Beauty was out there, all alone!"

"She was dead. Best ending for her."

I said nothing for a moment. I wondered what the hell planet he was on.

"You holdin' it against her?" His tone turned incredulous.

"I take a dim view of murder, yes."

"Not murder. Mercy."

"Murder. And fuck you, Judd. Fuck you, and the horse you rode in on."

"They've set her bail at one million."

Another pause. I watched Cherise sweeping the kitchen floor, Beauty playfully trying to chomp the bristles on the broom.

She stopped and looked at me.

"And?" I said into the phone, venom dripping from my voice.

"I ain't got that kind of money, Colby."

"Neither do I."

"Oh, my God. Yes, you do. You can help her. You can get her out."

"Not a chance."

"What?"

"I hope they arrest you, too, as an accessory after the fact."

He gasped on the other end of the phone. "That's a rotten thing to say."

"I could come up with worse, but you're a waste of my time."

"You're really not gonna bail her out?"

I hung up on him. Ten seconds later my phone rang again. I would have let it go to voice mail, except that I saw Detective Duchesne's number on the screen. The rumble of a motorbike outside made me think it had to be Duchesne out there.

"You gonna let me in, or what?" he asked when I took the call. "Your goons are out here lookin' real menacing."

I ended the call and walked to the front of the house, Beauty at my heels. Nuts and Marcel were both at the front door. Duchesne left his chopper near the front porch and nodded at Nuts and Marcel as he entered the house.

Nuts nodded back, but Marcel was acting funny though, slicking his hair back when he thought nobody was looking. He spat into his hand a couple of times, smoothing his unruly locks.

Whatever.

I noticed a frisson of something shimmer between Marcel and Duchesne. Were they falling for each other, or were they planning a duel at dawn? I couldn't tell which.

"Hey," I said to Duchesne as he squeezed his way past the two men. "Come on in."

"I figured you were up," Duchesne said. I was trying to decide how he'd found me.

"I called Diego when I couldn't locate you." He glanced around. "He said this was his safe house. Not bad. Said he fixed it up himself."

In the kitchen, Cherise poured fresh juice for everyone. Beauty kept hurling herself on her back for anyone who looked like they were good for a tummy rub. I wondered where she got her dating technique from and if it would work for me the next time I saw Diego.

"We got June Gold in custody. We're going after her husband, too." Duchesne sniffed his juice suspiciously.

"As an accessory after the fact?"

"No. Though we might tack that on for good measure." He knew he had our attention. "The U.S. Marshals just took him into custody. Your brother-in-law was arrested on an outstanding warrant stemming back to nineteen ninety-nine."

"Nineteen ninety-nine?" I thought back a moment. He met June Gold early in the spring of 2006, right after she and I moved to New Orleans.

"He killed a man. Gruesome homicide in Tempe, Arizona." Duchesne gave Marcel an appreciative glance. "Your friend here recognized him from a TV show." He leaned toward Marcel and shook his hand.

I thought neither man would let go for a moment.

"A TV show?" I was echoing everything Duchesne told me.

Marcel went pink around the cheeks. His damp curls hung around his ears and forehead giving him an almost angelic look. "Yeah. I saw it on one of those forensic shows.

Must have been about five years old, that thing. Saw it late at night. If it hadn't involved a child, I wouldn't have said anything." He shot an apprehensive glance at Duchesne.

"A child?" Man, this inclination to repeat everything was worse than having hiccups.

Duchesne nodded. "Judd's real name is James Atcherson. He killed his brother-in-law and nephew and tried to make it look like a home invasion robbery."

"Why did he do that?" Cherise asked. She'd turned pale.

"He had a sister, and the two of them were left their parents' home in Tempe. The sister had cancer and died. She'd left her share of the house and, apparently, a shitload of money to her husband and kid. He figured if he got rid of the brother-in-law and nephew, everything would revert to him. He might have gotten away with it except the police figured it out. He disappeared, changed his name, and his appearance. Lost a lot of weight. He's gotten away with it for all these years."

"If he looked so different, how did you know it was him?" I asked Marcel.

"I got good eyes. And besides. He's put on weight lately. I saw that TV show and I knew it was him."

"Thank you." I didn't know whether to hug him or shake his hand. I settled for a bit of both. When we broke away from each other, I said, "I wonder if June knew."

Duchesne looked at me. "She says not. He says she did."

"They're both assholes," I blurted. "What about the kids, Garnet Beauty, and Henry?"

"Children and Family Services has them. Your sister is in lockup at the downtown Louisiana Correctional Institute for Women. Judd, or should I say, James, is on his way to Federal custody at the Elayn Hunt Correctional Center pending extradition to Phoenix, Arizona. I can put you in touch with CFS about bringing the kids home to you, but there will have to be a hearing."

"I understand." My head was spinning. I was trying to get used to the idea that Judd wasn't Judd and that he was a cold-blooded killer. "Did he really murder his nephew?"

Duchesne nodded, sipping his juice. He looked surprised. "Say, this is pretty tasty."

"Of course it is." Cherise looked a little offended. "You think I can't cook?"

I kept thinking of my sister and her baking expertise. I couldn't believe the latest developments. As for Judd. Wow. That just beat everything.

"You're a great cook," Duchesne said. He glanced back at me. "Judd staged a home invasion at his sister's home. He was pissed the parents gave her money as well as half the house. He tied up and tortured his brother-in-law for hours. He stabbed and shot the nephew to make the guy talk. It was gruesome. He killed them both, but cut himself in the process, leaving a trail of blood at the scene. That's how the investigators figured it was him. They hauled him in for questioning. He had cuts on his hands. Guys who stab often miss and cut themselves." He shook his head. "He took off when he was left in an interview room that had a broken lock."

I kept trying to process what I'd heard. I'd hardly had time to digest this when he said, "Calvin turned himself in. He's the only one that seems upset. He—"

"He turned himself in?" That shocked me.

"Well, I don't think it was entirely his idea." Duchesne shook his head, an odd half-smile on his face. Marcel was doing the licking-smoothing thing again. "Calvin arrived, hands cuffed behind his back. Swore he'd come on his own but that's a hard way to travel, and he had some bumps and bruises on his face."

Diego had kept his word and found him for me.

"That just leaves your dad, and I think you and I should go talk to him, Colby."

I wasn't in a position to argue. I had no idea what Diego had told him and even if he had any notion that I knew where Cledus was. Besides, Duchesne had done a lot for me. He'd kept the search up for my sister when I was the only member of my family who wanted it. Having him present as I confronted my dad would stop me killing the old coot, too. I wanted Cledus to pay for his part in the crime. I wanted them all to pay.

"We should organize an attorney for you to represent you in family court," Duchesne said. "You should ask for an emergency hearing to get Garnet and Henry into your care."

"I know someone," Cherise said quickly. "Go find Cledus, I'll make some calls."

"Thanks." My cell phone rang as we were leaving. It was Jerry.

"Man, I woke up to CNN. June and Judd have been arrested. I had no idea he was an asshole, too."

"Yeah, I know, right?"

"What can I do to help?"

"I don't know yet."

"Are you going to get custody of the kids?"

"That's my plan."

"I suppose you heard about the crystal meth."

Cutting a glance toward Duchesne, I said, "No. Tell me."

"When they arrested June, she grabbed Judd and kissed him."

Where was he going with this? I caught Duchesne's gaze. He gave a signal to wrap up the conversation.

"Turns out she wasn't being romantic. She was slipping him a bag of crystal meth. They were just about to shoot up when the cops busted them."

"You saw this on the news?" Why hadn't Duchesne told

me anything about it?

"Yeah. They caught them on tape. One of the neighbors recorded it all on his cell phone."

Oh, man. I couldn't believe it. Every time I turned around, things just got worse and worse. I'd had no idea my sister had even been doing drugs. And ice of all things? I'd seen enough episodes of *Dog the Bounty Hunter* to know it's the most addictive drug on the face of the planet.

"Say, you remember John Sawicki, guy we used to run with?" Jerry asked.

"Some." I did recall him but couldn't think now what it was I knew about him. Then it all came back to me. He'd gone straight. Studied hard and wound up in the legal profession. Jerry and I had gone rogue.

"He has ads all over the radio and TV for custody cases."

"Wait," I said. "The guy with the toupee and the weird teeth?"

"That's the one. He called me. He remembered she was your sister. He's offering to represent you in court."

"Why would he do that?"

"Guess he's still got that crush on you."

Now I remembered. Jerry and I had been a clandestine item, and we'd met John. He'd fallen for me, but the feelings weren't reciprocated. I guess some guys are gluttons for punishment.

"You should let me and Mom help you," Jerry said. "I know you love Cherise, but the courts will want a stable home, and here at least they have one."

I hesitated. I did love Cherise.

"You can bring her and the dog," Jerry said. "Can I tell John to go ahead and contact CPS?"

"Yeah. Go ahead. And Jerry?"

"Yeah, bro?"

"Thanks."

"Por nada."

I ended the call. It wasn't nothing. It was huge. I told Cherise about John Sawicki and told her that once we got the kids, we would all go stay with Sue-Ellen.

"Oh, cool. I like her." She started to hum. "Besides, I'm starting to run out of juice. I think I might be getting sick of it."

I gave her a hug, bent down to ruffle my dog's head, and left with Duchesne. I caught Nuts' mournful glance. He was jealous. Wasn't a whole lot I could do about that right now.

"Look after them for me, will you?" I asked him over my shoulder.

He gave me a thumbs-up. His hair was looking really weird.

On his cell phone, Duchesne Googled the address for the place Diego said my dad was now being held. When we roared off to find him, I felt a momentary exhilaration as the wind whipped my face. I wished we could have kept driving.

I remembered a quote about riding motorbikes that goes like this: *meditation doesn't mean you have to sit still.* It's so true. Out on the road, my mind eased. I no longer wrestled with all the stuff that I'd been dealing with. The only thing my addled brain wanted to wrap itself around was Diego. He was my future. I was certain of it. Everything was damned wrong right now. But we could make it right. We would be a family. Me, Diego, the kids, and Cherise.

We could do it. I could see us in a big house. A big everything. Bikes, cars, a boat for the kids. An RV. Yeah. I could see us in an RV. I'd have to talk to Diego about that. All my childhood years, my dad's day job was selling RVs. He had one of the nation's original franchises. He was so busy selling the idea of the American Dream, of families sticking close, traveling the open road, that he forgot about me. He forgot about us.

I'd make sure Garnet and Henry felt safe, and loved, and . . . free.

As we neared the street where Cledus was being held, I wondered what I'd say. Duchesne roared to a stop.

"You'd better make this conversation short. I'm calling for backup. You have five minutes."

I walked into the house and could smell human piss.

"Your old man's wet the bed a couple of times," Stewart, a new prospect told me. "I think he's petrified."

He pushed open the bedroom door. I saw Cledus lying on a bed on his side, hands tied behind his back. My old man lifted his head and cracked a smile.

"There's my number one son," he said, sarcasm and bad breath pouring out between his yellow teeth.

Yeah, right.

I stood at the foot of the bed. "The police are on their way."

Fear lit his eyes.

"Don't worry. I'm not gonna hurt you, Dad." It had been a long time since I'd called him that. He'd lost the right to the name, to all my respect, after years of physically and mentally abusing me. Memories flooded back. I wanted to smother him with the pillow under his head, screaming my sister's name into the abyss.

"Why did you do it?" I asked. That's all it came down to. Why he let my sister die.

He let out an aggrieved sigh. "Your mom and me, we were okay until she had Garnet." His head sagged against the pillow. "She tipped Evangeline over the edge." He went silent for a moment. "No. Actually, she sent her right over the fucking cliff."

"You're blaming my sister for being born?"

His eyes filled with rage and his head came off the pillow.

"Evangeline and me, we had a good thing going until you came along. Then June and, fuck me, she went and got knocked up a third time. We discussed adopting Garnet Beauty out, but . . ."

He waited a beat. "Things were never the same after Garnet came. Your mama left me. Me. Shit, I still can't believe it. She left me with you." He spat out the word. I realized then how much he hated me. He hated us all. Had he ever loved anybody?

"Garnet being dead was an unfortunate, but acceptable loss." His tone was calm, his face defiant.

"She wasn't a used RV being returned to the lot, Dad. She was our baby."

"She was a little asshole. Jes' like the rest a yer." When he was being real, when he was being himself, Cledus lapsed into country-speak.

The old man went silent once again, the words, now said, unable to be taken back. He lay, looking off into the middle distance, blinking. I couldn't tell if he'd regretted his honesty, or whether he was working himself up to saying something much worse.

I waited.

He'd really aged. He'd given me his best shot. I leaned forward just as the police arrived. I heard the wail of sirens. Then came the knock at the door.

"You've lost your panache, old man. You got no style. You got no class. You're just an old bed wetter. Hope you enjoy prison. And by the way, seeing you get carted away to your destiny, now that's what I call an unfortunate, but acceptable loss. You're a prick, Cledus Young. I am no longer your son. I hate you more than I could ever hate a human being. I hope you die in pain."

I opened the door and waved my hand toward him, swallowing back the tears that threatened to overtake me.

"You okay?" Duchesne asked me.

I nodded.

"Wait for me out front. I'll get you back to the house."

It didn't take long. I rolled my eyes when I saw my father led out, the old man sniveling about how he was old and sick. He looked over at me.

"Your time will come, yer little fart." I looked away from him, knowing I'd never see him again, not even at his funeral.

"Fuck off, you old coot," I said and let them haul him away in a van.

Duchesne dropped me off back at the woods.

"Place looks dark," he said, as I hopped off the bike. "Sure you don't want me to come in there with you?"

"Naw. I know you want to go process Cledus."

"Naw. I want to go laugh in his face. I wanna make sure he gets put in a cell with some nice guy named Bubba. I know that old man mistreated you, Colby. I know he abused you. I'll put in a good word for you with CPS." He cut the engine. "I got a call while I was waiting for you outside. That idiot Judd, he swallowed the crystal meth your sister passed him. He almost died. He's been in the hospital having his stomach pumped. He's under armed guard. Tomorrow, he'll get shipped off to Arizona."

"Good. I hate to see the taxpayers pay his bills from now on, but I don't think justice will be served if he dies."

"Neither do I." He started the chopper up again. "Talk to you tomorrow." He zoomed off, and I walked through the trees. He was right. The place was dark.

Shit. I shoulda known better. I heard a crackle of twigs. Gunshots, and somebody said at my ear, "Don't move."

CHAPTER EIGHT

Diego

I backed up Chase's bike and roared off down the road. Cledus had told me that the name of Gilles' girlfriend was Lacy Grey. I figured the old man didn't have enough imagination to make up a name that lame. Most likely the name had been legally changed, and Lacy was as 'girlie' as it gets, next to Cherry and Candy. Ms. Grey, I learned, seemed to have done quite well for herself. Gilles had apparently given her quite a hefty sum of money before they sent him-her to the joint. Ms. Grey, formerly a female impersonator, was now the proprietor of a trendy beauty center called Lacy Lovely. It was tucked away on one of those little side streets in between a high-end clothing boutique and a foot clinic.

I parked Chase's bike across the street, tucked my vest away, and decided that with my jeans and navy T-shirt, I looked like any ordinary guy. I walked into Lacy Lovely and was frankly quite impressed. Facials, hair styling, makeup application, manicures, and something lethal going on behind a curtain with what sounded like a buzz saw. There were several people fussing over various clients, and I was pretty sure that some of those "ladies" were not.

A young girl sat at the desk. When I walked in, she gawked at me. "Hello," I said.

"Hello." She blinked. "You want a café mocha?"

That was an odd thing to ask. "No thanks. I'm looking for the owner. Is she here?"

"Oh sorry," she said. "I thought you were here to pick up someone. You're him, aren't you?"

"I beg your pardon?"

"The new BF. She told us all about you, said you're really good in bed."

"She did? That's good."

"She said you would protect her from that . . ." She lowered her voice. "Asshole. Her ex."

"Gilles Lafleur."

"Yeah, that guy. He's a mean bastard, wears a patch over one eye. Spooky. Guess you know he gave Lacy a fat lip."

"Shit." I took a breath. "So, you're right, I'm him, the boyfriend. Where is Ms . . . ah . . . Lacy, right now?"

"She's at home of course. She'd never been seen alive with that lip of hers. Even our best makeup doesn't cover it."

I stood there. Some of the patrons were looking at me curiously. I smiled.

"Aren't you going upstairs to see Lacy?"

"Ah, yeah." I nodded. "Sure."

"You can go through the back." She smiled. "You know, Lacy never said you were that good-looking, and young. Honey, you can't be more than thirty."

"I'm very mature for my age." I nodded to the ladies and walked by the counter. I hoped to hell I was headed the right way. No one said anything, so I kept going until I saw a door leading into a corridor.

I found a flight of stairs. I had a bad feeling as I climbed them, a real bad feeling. There was a door at the top of the stairs, and it was ajar. I edged closer. I wasn't going in there. "Ms. Grey?" I called out.

No answer. I took out my gun. "Ms. Grey? Ah, Lacy, are you in there?"

Nothing. I stuck out the toe of my boot and pushed the door all the way open. That's when I saw the body lying on the floor. There was blood everywhere. "Damn, what an animal."

I hurried back down the stairs and saw a fire exit. I slipped outside and then went around to the front. I crossed the road and hopped on the bike. I sat there. Ms. Grey wasn't going to help me find Lafleur. I could do the bars, ask some questions, but that was a waste of time. So I sat and watched the shop. That girl had said Lacy had a new boyfriend. I wondered who the guy was.

I was just about to leave when I saw a car drive up. It was a nice car, a blue sedan. A chauffeur got out and opened the door for a big, Creole man, dressed to the nines. I recognized him. That was Jefro Evans. The guy had major mob connections, owned a string of Jazz clubs. Was he the boyfriend?

I watched. It wasn't long after he went inside that I heard screaming. I sat back, waited. Evans came out fuming. He marched up and down on the sidewalk in front of the shop, hands flailing. His driver was doing his best to comfort him. Ladies were rushing out of the place, some of them with curlers in their hair.

The police would be here soon. I had little time to waste. I got off the bike and slowly crossed the street. "Mr. Evans?" I said.

He turned and looked at me, his face wet with tears. "What do you want? This is no time, boy."

"I know who killed that lady up there."

His eyes widened. He reached out to grab me, fist poised, but I put out my hand and stopped him.

"Who are you?"

"Diego Champagne," I told him.

He lowered his fist. "Leader of the Banni?"

"That's right."

"It was that bastard no good, one-eyed, ex-boyfriend of hers that killed her. He's fresh outta the joint."

"Gilles Lafleur."

"You know him? That son of a bitch. I even paid him off to leave her alone. Set him up last night in a high stakes poker game."

"Can you tell me where he is now?"

"Maybe I can but what does the Banni want with him?"

"Not the Banni, just me. Gilles and I have some unfinished business."

"What kind of business?" He eyed me.

"You know that patch he's wearing? I'm the cause."

"Damn. Well, I could tell you where he's at but killing him is my job."

"Okay. Fair enough. Tell me where to find him and, I promise you, I'll leave just enough life in him for you to snuff it out."

"You'll call me and tell me where to find him when you're finished?"

"It's a deal."

"He's most likely still in the game if he hasn't folded. They've been playing all night in a basement apartment over on the west side." He motioned to his driver. "Get me a pen and paper."

I waited as he jotted down the address, then handed it to me. "My number is on there."

"Okay." I glanced at it and put it into my pocket. "How many we talkin'?"

"Only four. Entry price is too high. You better punish him for what he's done, Champagne," Evans hissed. "I wanna know he felt pain before I wipe him off this earth."

I nodded. "You don't have to worry about that." I walked back to Chase's bike. The poker game was not more than a few miles away. I was hungry but decided to hold off on the meal until after I dealt with Lafleur.

As I parked across the street from the building where

Lafleur was playing his last game of poker, I didn't think that maybe I could lose.

I couldn't, because Colby wouldn't be able to handle any more heartache than he already had, and I knew he'd grieve if I died.

I walked on the grass and around to the side of the building. Some old lady on the second-floor balcony was staring down at me. I smiled up at her. "Forgot my key," I said, then put a finger to my lips. All I needed were the cops to show up. She went inside.

The window was easy to get off. I removed it and the screen and slipped through quietly to the floor. I was in a bedroom. I could hear sounds coming from the other room. I walked to the open door, took my gun out of my belt, and stepped out into the hallway. I moved silently to the kitchen where I could hear the sounds. They were in a kitchen. The room was thick with smoke, and I smelled whiskey and sweat.

I slid against the wall and waited for the right moment. I thought of Colby for a minute, and how much I loved him. I did love him, and I realized that I'd loved no one before him, and there would be no one after him. I wondered what kind of promises I could make to myself, or to him. I would like to tell him that everything was going to be different after I took care of Lafleur. But I wasn't sure even I could get myself to believe that. There was too much blood on my hands, too much shit and dirt. This life wasn't for Colby. He needed stability, a place to raise his niece and nephew, somewhere far from . . . me. For just a fleeting second, I almost decided to put down the gun and walk out of there, let Lafleur finish it, finish me. Colby would take care of my mother. He'd deal with the grief. He'd change his life and—

I heard something, then I saw a flash. I hit the floor, and the kitchen door flew open. Three really ugly guys walked in with submachine guns. I crawled down the hallway. They didn't know I was there. I wanted to keep it that way. I heard someone say they'd come for the money.

I got back into the bedroom and hightailed it out the window. I stood against the wall of the building and scanned everything. Chase's bike was still there across the road. There was a white van parked in front of it. Shit. I heard an exchange of fire. I focused on the bike. Could I make it before they came out again? If I stayed here, they'd see me.

I heard a noise above me. That little old lady came out on the balcony. I glanced up at her. "Don't make a sound," I told her as softly as I could.

She nodded.

"Can I . . . come up?"

She nodded.

I grabbed the floor of her balcony and pulled myself up. I crawled over the railing, took her arm and steered her back inside. I closed the door, took her into the bathroom where there was no window. She was scared. "Don't move. Stay here, okay?"

She nodded again. "Okay."

"They'll go if we wait."

She looked at my gun.

I hid it at my side. "Stay here." I carefully moved toward the balcony. I saw them run across the road and get into the van. They backed up, hit Chase's bike and sped off. "Shit," I said. "Chase is going to freak."

I went back to the bathroom. "It's all right. Wait five minutes and then call the police, okay?"

She nodded.

I left by her door and took the stairs down to the basement. I stopped, listened to see if I could hear anything. Nothing. I opened the door slowly and walked in. I dreaded what I'd find in the kitchen. Gun drawn, I entered.

I found only three men, all of them dead. Two were slumped at the table, and one was on the floor. None of the men were Gilles Lafleur. Then I realized why. Gilles Lafleur had orchestrated all of this. Guess he wasn't much of a card player.

I left the apartment, walked over to what was left of Chase's bike, and pulled out my phone. One of the prospects, a guy called Roga, picked up on the second ring. "Hey."

"Hey. I need a ride." I started to walk toward downtown. I heard the sirens in the distance. I told him the name of a diner I liked, which was a few blocks away, and he said he was on his way.

I gave Evans a call and gave him the bad news once I had a beer in front of me.

"You lost the fucker?"

"Yeah, but we have a date tonight." I told him to come by the Banni scrapyard after midnight, and he could finish him then.

I ordered blackened fish and rice and was on my second glass of beer when the prospect showed up. "So where's Chase's bike?"

"Don't ask. Wanna beer?"

"Pizza." He hunkered down in the booth across from me.

I grinned. "It's on me."

"Save some dough. Chase is going to freak. He'll want a custom-made bike."

"He'll get his bike."

"You get Lafleur?"

"Dance is still on."

"Fuck."

"It's okay. I could use some sleep."

We finished eating, and the prospect drove me back to the clubhouse. I locked myself in one of the rooms and slept. I didn't wake up until almost eleven p.m. I took a shower, changed my clothes and headed out the back way. No one saw me leave. I took one of the best bikes from the shop.

I drove out to the outer end of the scrapyard and waited. At around twelve-twenty, a car drove up. It stopped a few feet away from me. I got off the bike and stood there, waiting. I hadn't been prepared for what I'd feel when I saw him again. He'd aged a lot. He must have been pushing sixty, and his hair had gone white, contrasting with the black patch that covered his right eye.

I clenched my fists. This was the one who had taken everything from me, changed my life completely. Did I want to kill him? Yes, I guess I did. For all the touchdowns I'd never make, all the fields I'd never run across again with a football in my hand.

"Hello, Diego," he said. He took a few steps.

I glanced past him. "You didn't come alone."

"No. In fact, I brought a friend of yours."

I stiffened.

"Bring him out, Jose."

When I saw Colby, I thought I'd die. There was a short little bastard standing beside him with a gun. Colby's hands were tied behind his back, but he seemed unhurt. "Where's my mother?" I demanded.

"She's fine. I wouldn't hurt a sick lady. I left her in that little love nest you built. Nuts and Marcel however . . . well . . . they died bravely."

"You fucker."

He laughed.

"Let Colby go. He's got nothing to do with this."

"You're lovers. He's got everything to do with this. You need a cheering section."

"This was supposed to be you and me."

"Bring him over here." Lafleur motioned to his thug.

The man dragged Colby over to where Lafleur was standing. Colby hadn't said a word, but his gaze locked with mine.

"Now." Lafleur smiled. "I didn't feel like I could leave your mother alone, so I left one of my men behind to keep her company."

I narrowed my eyes.

"Before I finish something I should have finished years ago, I thought we'd play a little game."

I waited.

"It's kind of like Russian Roulette."

"Get to the point."

"Well." Lafleur smiled again. "You have a choice. One of them will need to die, this one here . . ." He pointed at Colby. "Or your dear mama. Heads you lose, tails you lose."

The thug pressed the gun to Colby's head. I saw him close his eyes.

"Choose, Diego. Or I'll choose for you," Lafleur said. "Now, I figure a mama gives you life and this one," he sneered, touching Colby's hair. "Gives your cock life. Which is more important to you, Diego, your mama, or your cock?" He held up his cell phone. "One call to my friend, and it's over."

"Who told you about that place? How did you know they were up there?"

"Not everyone loves you, Diego." He shrugged. "Anyone can be bribed."

Nuts. No. He'd never betray me. Who then? It didn't matter. I put up my hands. "Please, take me. Do what you want to me but let Colby and my mother go."

"Do what I want?" He looked like he was contemplating that. "That would be a dream. Your death will be slow and very painful. Might take days. And why should I trust you? You have a gun."

I took the gun out of my belt and tossed it on the ground. "Take me."

Colby was shaking his head. "No," he shouted.

Lafleur glanced at him. "I think he really loves you."

"Call that guy with my mother and tell him to leave her alone, release Colby, and I'll go with you now. Come on, Lafleur, they mean nothing to you. You want me. Take me."

He smiled, nodded at his thug. "Take him back up to the cabin and tell Austin to leave."

I took a breath.

The thug was dragging Colby back to the car. He turned to look at me. "Diego?"

I didn't look at him. I couldn't.

Lafleur walked over to where I stood and picked up the gun. I had one chance. As he leaned over, I moved forward and kicked him hard in the head. He flew back, and I scrambled for the gun. I shot up on my knees and fired at Lafleur. I hit him in the chest. By the car, Colby was struggling with that thug. I ran over to them, grabbed the guy and hit him so hard, it knocked him out cold. Lafleur was hit in the shoulder. He fired at us but missed. I dragged Colby behind the vehicle while Lafleur crawled behind one of the cars.

I untied Colby's hands. He reached out and grabbed the thug's gun, which lay nearby. I touched his hair and kissed his forehead quickly. "Stay here. I'm going after him."

"No." He grabbed my arm and held on for dear life. "No."

"Colby, it's okay. It's okay."

He was shaking like a leaf.

"If you see a car, it's probably Evans. Don't worry, he's no friend of Lafleur's. But if anyone comes near you and you don't like them, shoot them."

He tried to smile. I handed him my cell phone. "Call and make sure Mama is okay. Send someone out there."

"Okay." He nodded. I raced out from behind the car and entered the labyrinth of metal scraps. It was dark, and I couldn't see very much. I could make out the shadows and movement though, and I could follow the blood. Lafleur had lost a lot of it.

I heard the sound of an engine and realized that it was probably Evans. I wanted to get to Lafleur before he did. I rounded the corner and stopped. Lafleur was lying there, the gun in his hand. He hardly had enough strength to hold it, but it was pointed at me. "It's over," I told him.

"No. You die and then it's over. I don't care if I die now, but you're coming with me."

"Shoot, then. Get it over with. You took my life back then by smashing my knees."

"Yeah, I know. I saw you play. I made sure you wouldn't play again." He started to laugh.

That was it. I made a lunge for him. The gun went off and, as we struggled, I knew Lafleur was dying. I could hear the rasp. I didn't realize I was hit until he took his last breath. There was a lot of blood. I assumed it was his.

I heard the sound of running feet. Evans and his driver and Colby. Everything swam around me. I was on my knees. Colby got on his. I heard him say, "No, no, no, please, no." I heard him whisper in my ear something about an ambulance.

I shook my head. "No, no ambulance," I grunted. "I'll go to jail. I don't want to . . ." I was struggling to stay conscious. I couldn't let them take me.

Evans took control. "We'll take care of the body, and we'll get him to the clubhouse. We'll get him a doctor that knows how to keep their mouth shut." He peered down at me. "Okay, Diego. Hold on."

I nodded. I think I tried to thank him. And that was it. I fell forward, saved from hitting the ground by Colby's arms.

I don't know how long I was out. When I opened my eyes, my mother was sitting beside me, looking worse than I did. Colby was standing behind her looking anxious.

"You awake, child?" she asked me.

I managed to nod. "Yeah."

"Good. Why'd you have to go and worry us half to death? We thought you were dying."

"I'm sorry." I smiled.

"Not good enough." She looked at Colby. "I'll be back. You got some explaining to do to this boy here."

She left the room.

Colby leaned down and kissed my forehead. "Damn you, Diego," he whispered. "You almost died. If it hadn't been for that doctor Evans got. How do you feel?"

"Tired. Am I missing any parts?"

"Nothing important." He grinned. His hand slipped down to my cock under the blanket. "Yep, still there."

I laughed. It hurt. "Stop that now."

"Don't worry about anything. Listen, Nuts and Marcel made it. Good thing, too. I think Nuts and Duchesne might be sweet on each other."

"Where am I?"

"At your cabin in the woods."

"So we've got a house full of invalids?"

He nodded. "We got you all hospital beds. Doctor will be back tomorrow."

"Who was the traitor?"

He shook his head. "We don't know yet. Don't worry about that now."

"It's all I'm going to think about."

"Diego," he said softly. He stroked my face.

"What?"

"I have a good chance to get the kids if . . . well . . . I have to prove I have a job and—"

"I'll take care of it."

"I can live here but —"

"No." I took a breath. Damn, that was painful. "Where did he get me?"

"In the chest, missed the heart by a few inches. You were lucky."

"Not so lucky," I said softly.

"I don't want to leave you."

"But you will." I met his eyes. "It's got to be, Colby. Those kids need you. Is your old man in custody?"

"Yes."

"Did he tell you what you needed to know?"

Colby nodded. "I'll tell you one day when I'm able."

I smiled and nodded. "I'm going to talk to some people tonight. I'll set you up anywhere you want. Just tell Chase. We'll open a little business for you."

"No. I'm taking over June Gold's bakery. Sue-Ellen and Jerry are going to help me. I think Cherise should move in with us."

"You know anything about baking?"

"Nope. Can't even boil an egg. The attorney I'm working with doesn't think my pool hall is a reputable enough job. I'm gonna have to quit the Banni, Diego, or at least look like I am."

I shifted on the bed. "You won't ever have to the see the Banni, I'll make sure no one ever knows of your association with us, and none of us will ever come near those kids. We can't risk that. Child services could take them away."

The tears filled his eyes. He didn't speak. He just nodded.

I took his hand, squeezed it. "Okay?" I saw him swallow hard.

"I almost lost my mind when I thought you were dying. How am I supposed to live without you?"

"You'll learn to. The kids will —" I stopped, contemplated

my life without Colby. "It will be okay. Listen, we were never supposed to be together. It's always been impossible, hasn't it?"

He didn't answer. He just said, "I'm not leaving until you're better."

"Yes, you are. No more 'one last time,' okay? I don't think I could do it. And those kids are waiting for you." I turned my head away.

Colby laid his head on my chest and sobbed without making a sound. Only the motion of his body gave him away. The tears ran down my cheeks, but I didn't look at him. I couldn't because if I did, I knew I'd beg him to stay. After a few minutes, he quietly left the room.

Alone again. Naturally.

YOU MAY ALSO ENJOY THE FOLLOWING FROM EXTASY BOOKS INC:

Permanent Moonlight
A. J. Llewellyn and D. J. Manly

Excerpt

The scene in front of my eyes was flooded with cops. They seemed to swarm around me like a bunch of menacing bees. Cops made me uneasy, especially if there was an army of them. And I was really upset by all this on all kinds of levels, the murders, the word scrawled in blood, but especially the missing kids.

Colby had called his cop friend, Duchesne, and he'd come running as usual. I was pretty sure he was half in love with Colby, but I'd never tell Colby that. He'd say I was jealous. Maybe I was. I wanted to comfort him, but I kept my distance.

The cops knew who I was, and of course, they eyed me suspiciously, even though I'd taken off my vest and was holding it in my hand. One of them, a big, burly fellow with a brush cut kept looking at me as if he either wanted to fuck me or throw me in a jail cell. My money was on the latter scenario.

I should have left before the army of emergency vehicles

arrived, but Colby was upset over the kids. I knew he wanted me to wait with him. As soon as I saw the cops, I got out
of the way. Right now the dead wagon was carrying out
bodies. Jesus. This is unreal.

Colby stood a few feet away, talking to Duchesne, who
seemed at a loss for words. He kept hugging Colby, which
bugged me since I'd been told he liked men, Nuts, in partic-
ular. He must have liked pistachios a lot to put up with
Nuts' crazy habits. A car pulling up to the curb across the
street distracted me from that thought. A man got out of a
dark Plymouth. I couldn't help but notice. He was gro-
tesquely obese and short, no more than around five-foot-
five. A mop of red hair fell over his forehead, and I could see
that his big round face was smattered with freckles. He wore
a grey suit with a white shirt. Honestly, he looked like some
kind of beached whale. He came to stand a few feet from me.
He surveyed the scene for a moment then he looked over at
me. He approached me as if it was some kind of a challenge,
his chest puffed out. He lifted his chin as he waddled toward
me.

"There you are," he announced. "What are you still doing
here I wonder?"

I looked down at him. He didn't even come to my shoulder. His green eyes were shiny like a snake's. "Who might
you be?"

"My name is Elmer Flint." He flashed his card. "DCFS."
He didn't offer his hand. "And of course, we all know who
you are."

I lifted an eyebrow. "We do?"

"They told me you were a smart mouth."

"Who are they?"

"You didn't answer my question. What would the leader
of the Banni be doing here at a crime scene?"

"I'm a concerned citizen."

He laughed. "Right." He glanced at Colby. "He'll lose
those children if you don't back off. Leave him alone, Diego,

and let him raise those kids in a decent, God-fearing environment."

God-fearing environment? WTF. "You found the kids then?"

"We have them, yes. They were brought to DCFS an hour ago."

"By whom?"

"This isn't your concern or the concern of the Banni."

I took a step toward Colby. I intended to relieve his mind about the kids.

The DCFS guy put a hand on my forearm.

I glanced at him. "I don't recommend you touch me."

He removed his hand and took a step back. He had the good sense to look scared for a second. "The police will tell him shortly."

"What about the minister's kids?"

"Safe."

I breathed a sigh of relief.

"You really put on a good show." He brushed something imaginary off the front of his lapel. "Do you actually care about him and those kids? I mean, as much as someone the likes of you can care about anything or anyone."

"What do you think?"

"I think somewhere deep down in that tough, cool exterior, you might. So, back off." He met my gaze.

"Who in the fuck are you really?" I gritted my teeth.

"Can't you read?" He went to take out his card again.

I clenched my fist. "Yes, I can fuckin' read."

He put the card back in his pocket. "You know what I mean."

"Whose cock-sucker are you?"

He gave me a cold smile. "You'd know more about sucking cock than I would."

My jaw tightened.

"You really want to hit me right now. It's not easy holding back, is it, Diego?" He smiled. "Go ahead." He looked around. "We're surrounded by cops."

I took a breath and unclenched my fist. "Lucky break for you."

"Not a break. I know you're much smarter than that. Actually, you're the smartest leader the Banni has ever had. Too bad, you're going to wind up dead. It won't be much longer now."

"That sounds like a threat," I said, watching as a police officer walked over to talk to Colby. They were telling him the kids were all right.

Colby looked at me, utter relief on his face.

I looked away.

"Who are your friends?" I asked the man beside me.

"That's my business. Let's just say that as long as Colby stays away from bad influences like you, he'll have those kids. If he loses them, he'll have only you to thank. I wonder how much he'll want you then, the man who made him lose those kids. You want to be responsible for that, Champagne? Is it worth a fast fuck? Anyway, Colby will deal. You can't be that good in bed."

"How would you know?" I met his gaze.

He didn't reply.

I sneered at him.

I was sure the Texas Crushers or the mob were responsible for this. The mob's probably already muscling in on the drug action with the Crushers. It wasn't enough for those bastards to have a piece of the drug pie, they wanted it all now. I'd tried to make peace between us. Damn it. I knew it wouldn't last, not with all that money up for grabs. Badger was so damn weak. He'd made a deal with the devil, the Texas Mafia. Everyone would pay now.

"There's a contract on me," I said, folding my arms across my chest.

"You're never getting out of the Banni, Diego, unless it's in a box."

I nodded. "Now tell me something I don't know."

"I suggest this little conversation stays between us. Colby has enough to worry about with those kids. He's out now. Don't drag him back down into the dirt with you."

"Who else knows about Colby and me?"

"Your soldiers all think you're God's gift to women. I suggest you fuck that little girlfriend you keep on a string more often. She says you're one hell of a lover."

Tammy?

"There's a stool in my club. Who is it?"

No answer. I turned my head to look at Flint, and he was already on his way over to Colby. I watched him as he introduced himself and shook hands.

Colby loved those kids so much. He'd just buried his sister, and the other one was in prison. I couldn't mess it up for him. Didn't matter how much I loved him. And now there was a price on my head. If the Crushers or the mob wanted to get to me, they would eventually. But before they threw dirt over me, I was going to find out who had betrayed me and how in hell they knew that Colby and I were lovers.

ABOUT THE AUTHOR

A.J. Llewellyn is the author of almost three hundred published gay romance novels. A.J. lives in California, but dreams of living in Hawaii. Frequent trips to all the islands, bags of Kona coffee in the fridge and a healthy collection of Hawaiian records keep A.J. refueled.

A.J's passion for the islands led to writing a play about the last ruling monarch of Hawaii, Queen Lili'uokalani. A.J. has written a non-erotic novel about the overthrow of her kingdom written in diary form from her maid's point of view.

A.J. never lacks inspiration for male/male erotic romances and has to prise fingers from the computer keyboard to pursue other passions: collecting books on Hawaiiana, surfing and spending time with family, friends and animal companions.

D.J. Manly: I write not only for my own pleasure but for the pleasure of my readers. I can't remember a time in my life when I haven't written and told stories. When I'm not writing, I'm dreaming about writing, doing something wild and adventurous, or trying to make the world a better and more open-minded place to live in. I adore beautiful men, and I know I'm not alone in this! Eroticism between consenting adults, in all its many forms, is the icing on the cake of life!

D.J. has published well over two-hundred novels/novellas and is a well-seasoned writer.

www.ingramcontent.com/pod-product-compliance
Lightning Source LLC
Chambersburg PA
CBHW060831120626
46557CB00001B/464